*KATE O'BRIEN*

974) was born in Limerick, Ireland, the fourth daughter of
Thornhill and Thomas O'Brien. Her mother died when she
nd she was educated at Laurel Hill Convent, Limerick, and at
y College, Dublin. Kate O'Brien lived in London for some
where she made her living as a journalist and began to write
nd plays. She also worked in Manchester, on the *Guardian*, and
ar as a governess in Spain: a country she was to return to and
often.

Brien originally became known as a playwright, her first
ing *Distinguished Villa* (1926) and *The Bridge* (1927). But it
the publication of her first novel, *Without My Cloak* (1931),
work became widely acclaimed. Described by J. B. Priestly as
cularly beautiful and arresting piece of fiction", it won the
rnden and the James Tait Black Prizes of 1931. This was
d by eight more novels: *The Ante-Room* (1934), *Mary Lavelle*
, *Pray for the Wanderer* (1938), *The Land of Spices* (1942), *The*
*Summer* (1943), *That Lady* (1946), *The Flower of May* (1953)
*Music and Splendour* (1958). Two of these novels, *Mary Lavelle*
*e Land of Spices*, were censored for their "immorality" by the
Censorship Board. Kate O'Brien dramatised three of her novels,
*Lady* also being made into a film starring Olivia De Havilland;
rote travel books: *Farewell Spain* (1937), and *My Ireland* (1962);
tobiography, *Presentation Parlour* (1963); English Diaries and
nals (1943) and a monograph on Teresa of Avila (1951). Her works
been translated into French, German, Spanish, Czech and
sh.

ter a brief marriage at the age of twenty-six Kate O'Brien
ained single for the rest of her life. In 1947 she was elected a
ber of the Irish Academy of Letters and a Fellow of the Royal
ety of Literature. She lived in Roundstone, County Galway until
when she moved to Boughton, near Faversham in Kent, where
died at the age of seventy-six.

her work Virago publish *Mary Lavelle*, *That Lady* and *Farewell*
*Spain*

# THAT LADY

## A NOVEL

### KATE O'BRIEN

With an Introduction by
**DESMOND HOGAN**

Virago

Published by VIRAGO PRESS Limited 1985
Reprinted 1988
A print on demand book published by Virago Press in 2004

First published by William Heinemann Ltd, London 1946

Virago edition offset from first edition

*British Library Cataloguing in Publication Data*

O'Brien, Kate
That Lady.
I. Title
823′.912[F]        PR6029.B65

ISBN 1 84408 194 X

**Virago Press**
**An Imprint of**
**Little, Brown Book Group**
**100 Victoria Embankment**
**London EC4Y 0DY**

www.virago.co.uk

# INTRODUCTION

Why did'st thou promise such a beauteous day
And make me travel forth without my cloak?

Between her birth in Boru House, Limerick, on 3 December 1897 and her death in the Kent and Canterbury Hospital, Canterbury, in the afternoon of 13 August 1974, Kate O'Brien chose discretion and privacy as a maxim for her life. In her last book, a book of reminiscences, *Presentation Parlour* (1963), Kate O'Brien piquantly refers to an aunt, a nun, who expressed a desire to read her first novel *Without My Cloak* (1931) and was only given it with certain sections pinned by safety pins. The nun was amply satisfied with her censored read. In a way when one comes to look at it, unlike like those of many authors, certain sections of Kate O'Brien's life are closed off from us by safety pins. To know a little more one must construct from the pointers in her fiction, from her few autobiographical writings; one asks her friends, one delicately handles an heirloom of photographs.

My favourite photograph of Kate is one of her in her twenties, about the time of her short-lived marriage, in a shapeless many-coloured jersey. She has a face that resembles someone she quoted in *English Diaries and Journals* (1943), Katherine Mansfield. A face that is both serene and yet dogged by the fact of exile. It is an image that is premature in a final reckoning with Kate O'Brien because the image of her that seems to survive is that of the author of *That Lady*; her public portrait was finally completed with the success of *That Lady*, a middle-aged woman still with a twenties-style hair cut, her impressively-boned Limerick face a little solemn, her eyes aristocratic,

challenging, but not arrogant. Having spent a while looking at Kate O'Brien's work my conclusion is that she was
incapable of arrogance. Her life, like her work, was a
supplication to a God who was partly provincial and
partly a global traveller.

In her life Kate O'Brien knew the vicissitudes of poverty
and wealth; she encountered international success and in
the latter part of her life on The Street, Boughton in Kent,
an eclipse from the public eye. In many ways the end of
*That Lady* was prophetic of the end of Kate O'Brien. As
Ana de Mendoza forfeits her Mantegna, a lifetime of
refinement enshrined in it, so we can presume Kate had to
relinquish her own precious works of art on selling her
house in Roundstone, Connemara, (a house recently
owned and vacated by Sting of the Police) and retiring to
Kent. But prior to this fate, as for Ana de Mendoza, the
mulberry trees had bloomed for Kate, the world of her
time had chattered about her, as in the cases of Rose and
Clare in *As Music and Splendour* she was more than
familiar with the "symbols and augurs of total success".

Kate O'Brien's grandfather was evicted from a small farm
just after the Famine; he headed towards Limerick city
where by the 1860s he had established a thriving horse
breeding business. In her first novel *Without My Cloak*, a
grand gesture of an Irish novel not unlike Eilís Dillon's
recent *Across the Bitter Sea*, Kate chronicled the emotional
lives of an Irish bourgeois family through the nineteenth
century. But Irish bourgeois families, as in the case of
Kate's own, very often have their roots in recent poverty
and catatonic acts of transcendance. Insecurity travels like
a banshee through such families. In her second novel *The
Ante-Room* (1934), a kind of *Lady Chatterly's Lover*
without the release of the sexual act, Kate very brilliantly,
very toughly denuded such a family of the romance and
left us with images of the detritus of the Irish bourgeois

family, the gardens, the garden-houses, the guns poised for suicide.

Kate's much-loved mother died when Kate was a child and she was sent to Laurel Hill Convent, run by the Faithful Companions of Jesus, which she left when she was eighteen. Kate loved the school, a school where Mother Thecla and the bishop were wont to converse in Latin in the garden, a school which bordered on the majesterial Shannon, and from it she coaxed the experience for her most perfect novel, *The Land of Spices* (1941), one of the most important smaller novels of the twentieth century. Youth is set against age. A girl on the threshold of life against a nun about to become Mother General of her order. There is love between nun and girl. But intercepting this love, in the nun's eyes, is an image of her father making love to a boy student in Brussels, a sight which initially drove her into the convent. The innocence of age and the innocence of youth is intercepted by an image of carnal love. The girl is walking into the world of such images. The nun is quietly withdrawing from the memory of the image. We can take it that Kate, on leaving Laurel Hill in June 1916, was walking into the world of these paradoxes, innocence inaugurated into experience. The nun was based on an English Reverend Mother who was at Laurel Hill in Kate's time, a woman who never smiled so alienated as she was by this grey city and this to her slovenly river, a woman of "Yorkshire bred and Stonyhurst men".

Already the duality of Ireland and England was established in Kate's personality. An American writers' directory of the 1940's tells us that on Kate's visit to the United States in the late forties she was without an Irish accent. I imagine those pinched "Stonyhurst" eyes looking with trepidation after Kate from a convent gate in 1916. Kate's father died in 1916. His business had already been in decline. In Dublin in her mackintosh "half starved by the holy men and the holy women" Kate walked among the ruins of an English-built city. An uncle of hers, Uncle Hickey, had wept when Queen Victoria, "our great little queen", had died. But Kate befriended many young and radiant revolutionaries at University College, a great number of whom, she tells us, had only a few years to live though that could not be suspected in a world which dazzled with ideas. Within a few years Kate had taken some of these ideas to Washington, working indirectly on behalf on the newly-declared Irish Free State, her American sojourn giving an authority to the final section of *Without My Cloak* in which Denis Considine hopelessly looks for his fugitive beloved in the half-lit late nineteenth-century world of port-side New York, a section where Kate, like some maverick folk-song writer, seems to have trapped all the acumen of an archetypal experience.

But before Washington Kate worked briefly on the *Manchester Guardian*, living in Manchester, and taught two terms at a London school. An incident there prepares us for the heroine of *Mary Lavelle* (1936). Kate's beauty and graciousness made such an impact on the girls she was teaching that a mother traipsed to the convent to see what was astir, to be met at the door by a nun who declared "Well the fact is the beloved is very beautiful." 1922–23 Kate was in another country. Spain. Which was to be the love of her life, a country from which she was barred from 1937 to 1957 for expressed Republican sympathies (*Farewell Spain*, 1937). In Bilbao in the rainy winter of 1922–23 Kate was acquainted with an Englishman who when she encountered him years later could only disdainfully recall the mud. Kate loved the mud for it reminded her of Ireland. In the Middle Ages there was constant commercial traffic between Spain and the West Coast of

Ireland. A dark people on the West Coast of Ireland, the street names of certain Irish towns—in Galway there are names like Madeira Street, Velasquez de Palmeira Boulevard—bear witness to this.

In 1922 Ireland had a new link with Spain. It exported governesses. Kate joined the misses, the "legions of the lost ones, the cohorts of the damned", the women who spoke English imperfectly and bided their time in cafés, hoping for the consummation of marriage. In *Mary Lavelle* there is a gesture of renunciation of Ireland, less publicised than Joyce's, but, for me, more tender, more universal. A young, already-betrothed, Irish governess, naked in the night, after seducing a young married Spaniard, realises she has sold "the orthodox code of her life", she has burnt her boats. "She would answer it, taking the consequences." Like Agnes in *The Ante-Room*, Clare in *As Music and Splendour*, Ana in *That Lady*. She accepts the lifelong totality of a single choice. In a way the night of lost virginity in *Mary Lavelle* dawns into the burning days under the Guadarramas in *That Lady*; Ana, older than Mary, still carries the struggle ensuing from the same choice. She knows she must let the consequences of her choice run their full gamut before she can connect again with her immortal soul. The landscape of Castile itself, eternal, unyielding, becomes a foil to the consternation within her. Mary in *Mary Lavelle* visits Castile for the first time and perceives it as "meeting place of Moor and monk", a land where the miracles of the New Testament could comfortably have taken place. Her persona as it is developed in the character of Ana de Mendoza is destined to seek the miracle of salvation here in spite of an adulterous affair she regards as a mortal sin.

In 1923 Kate married a young Dutch journalist in a registry office, cohabiting with him in a confined space in Belsize Park; often, Kate would recollect, the two would stroll in state into London, pretending it was for exercise, whereas in fact the real reason for these promenades was lack of money. The marriage lasted a year. *Distinguished Villa*, Kate's first play, produced in 1926, a study of the middle classes of Brixton, was very nearly a tremendous success but its run was ended by the General Strike. The British papers in 1932 were describing a remarkably comely Irish woman, whom many thought was just over from Limerick, going to collect the Hawthornden Prize. As long as English was so beautifully used by Irish people one paper gushed Ireland and England could never really be enemies. Kate's age was given as either thirty or thirty-one. In fact Kate's first novel *Without My Cloak* was published on her thirty-fourth brithday in December 1931. Kate's second two novels, *The Ante-Room* and *Mary Lavelle* are each a giddy leap ahead of the last. The first wavering of quality is her fourth novel *Pray for the Wanderer* (1938). But there is a remark that seems to have gathered force with the development of Kate's life. The hero, an expatriate Irish writer, briefly home on a visit to a grey, Southern, river-side city, reflects that "a life of absence predicates a life of absence".

Kate chose England for the war. During the war she published *The Land of Spices* and *The Last of Summer* (1943). Among the flying bombs she wrote her most structured novel, a novel which reveals itself like the panels of a painting, *That Lady*. Among the dramatic consternation of her time everything in the novel impels towards the inner life of Ana de Mendoza. She is a woman of middle age, the one-eyed, a little ridiculous looking, but to those who are intimate with her, magnetically sensual and emotionally calming. The post-war reading public loved her and *That Lady* sold more than half a million copies in its first few years of publication. The book was filmed. "I went to see it one afternoon" Kate says, "and there were lots of little boys in the cinema. They were booing and whistling and, of course, were absolutely right. I agreed with them and left the cinema."

On the proceeds from the book, film version, stage version Kate moved to Ireland; she was possessed by the old Celtic dream that one should die in Ireland; for her prospective burial she picked out a hill overlooking a beach near Roundstone. She purchased a house in Roundstone, one occasionally plagued by rats whom some local shop proprietors muttered were the Tuatha de Danann in disguise. But in spite of the magic of white beaches and mystic rats *The Flower of May* (1953), shows a diminishing of tension. Her next and last novel *As Music and Splendour* (1958), was not a success and though marred by languor it is iridescently memorable for its depiction of "complicated dusts and civilisations" and of lesbian love. Clare, a young Irish opera singer in Rome at the end of the last century, brings a Catholic sense of fidelity to a lesbian relationship only to be shattered to find that others are not inured to the same sense of fidelity even in something as extreme and as, to her, soul-risking as lesbian love. The end of Kate O'Brien's life in fiction is Clare walking into an uncertain and lonely life. A sense of sin, chosen and clung to, has a say in the last paragraph of *As Music and Splendour*.

Having sold her house in Roundstone in 1961 Kate moved to Boughton, near Faversham in Kent, where she secured a little house. In *The Ante-Room* an English doctor, Sir Godfrey Bartlett-Crowe, who realises that Dublin has at least a few good wine cellars in its favour, ventures into "the murderous and stormy South" to be taken aback by the elegance of the Mulqueen family. Sir Godfrey would have been equally surprised to find a member of such a family living in the South-East corner of England in the 1960s. Kate's family was always haunted by the fear of declining fortunes. Aunt Hickey, of Mespil Road Dublin, used to shopping in Switzers, on bankruptcy, trained her parrot to say "Damn Switzers" on which she would approve him "Good boy, Sam."

I don't know what Kate's attitude to her new relative obscurity was. Her books were following one another out of print. But she maintained a distinguished and acerbic poise in her column in *The Irish Times*. In *English Diaries and Journals* she quoted Katherine Mansfield "And when I say 'I fear' don't let it disturb you, dearest heart. We all fear when we are in waiting rooms. Yet we must pass beyond them, and if the other can keep calm, it is all the help we can give each other." One is reminded of the stolid devotion of Bernardina to Ana at the end, and of Ana's final isolation, from the world of glamour she was accustomed to, from the world of company, her last and only contact being her daughter. One is reminded of the anguish of Kate's last months in a hospital ward, deprived of her classical music and her Radio Four quiz programmes, forced to listen to the clatter of Radio One and Two. Two weeks after having a leg amputated she died. On her gravestone in Faversham cemetery is a simple epitaph from a childhood hymn of Kate's. 'Pray for the Wanderer.' In *The Flower of May* is a paragraph that compels with relevance.

Fanny looked about the beautiful wide table, at the gleaming glass and heavy silver, at the Sevres plates and dishes; she smelt and appraised the radiant fruits; she tasted her golden wine and looked with attention at the many splendid faces, ageing and young and very young, about her in the gentle lamplight. "It is a lovely scene," she thought, "all this civilisation, generosity and peace; all this blind, easy grace, this taking for granted of perfection in small things; all these radiant eyes, all this well-mannered affection, all this assurance, this polish, physical and even mental. But I belong to another place. I have dallied, I have dawdled. None of this is either mine or what I want. Mother, I am coming home.

Kate never finally got home or wanted to go home.

New Year 1969 Kate put these words in *The Irish Times*. "Private life remains—and cannot be taken away, except by death. Though, as Marvell reminded us very truly 'The grave's a fine and private place.'" *That Lady*, her most commercially successful novel, is about private life, Ana de Mendoza's attempt to preserve private emotions against the carnivorous demands of her society and her time and her attempt to preserve a knowledge of her soul against a passionate and very physical love affair. In *Teresa of Avila* (1951), Kate makes reference to a follower of Teresa, who after her death left his Carmelite order, and spent the rest of his life wandering as a tramp in North Africa. Ana de Mendoza is another such character. Her life a side-show of history. She stumbled out of "The Letters of Saint Teresa" for Kate, Teresa having had a run in with the princess. It is not the organisation of historical events and characters, the arabesque of place names that finally impresses but the imaginative totality Kate brings to the emotional life of Ana de Mendoza. Philip is the other character that is wholly palpable but despite his tangibility he is a wraithe-like character; time, the Nazis, what you will. Ana de Mendoza realises that once an action has begun—her affair—she must see it through against all other principles and when it has run its course she can connect again with the journey of her salvation. Not before. Kate O'Brien's theme can be summed up in two words. "Nunc Dimittis". The life of experience chosen and lived to the point you can say "Now I've lived; now experience has come to its logical conclusion and now I can tend again to the acreage of spiritual life within me and that alone."

Ana de Mendoza is a woman pitted against a time of manifold danger and much chaos; her reservoir of emotions is filled by the world her emotions must fight against; her triumph, and the book's, is that her persona transcends its time, its enemies, and time itself with the magnitude of its sensitivity and the depths of its intuitions. Ana is a child of any time when the idea of individuality is attacked, when inner life is under fire, when individuals must square up to the notions of their monomaniac kings. Ana's struggle against the king is, apart from anything else, a wonderful story; the king's final punishment a birth for her and a revelation for the reader. And the fact that Ana happens to be a sixteenth-century Spanish princess points Kate in the direction of lines by Marina Tsvetayeva:

> Back to the land of Dreams and Loneliness—
> Where we—are Majesties, and Highnesses.

*Desmond Hogan, London, 1984*

## FOREWORD

WHAT follows is not a historical novel. It is an invention arising from reflection on the curious external story of Ana de Mendoza and Philip II of Spain. Historians cannot explain the episode, and the attempt is not made in a work of fiction. All the personages in this book lived, and I have retained the historical outline of events in which they played a part; but everything which they say or write in my pages is invented, and—naturally—so are their thoughts and emotions. And in order to retain unity of invention I have refrained from grafting into my fiction any part of their recorded letters or observations.

KATE O'BRIEN.

## PROLOGUE. (October 1576)

### I

ANA did not wait for the king in the porch of her house. She stood above it, in her drawing-room, on the threshold of the central, balconied window. From there she could overlook the market-place, which was outside the open forecourt of her house, and she was spared the courtier-fuss of her son, Rodrigo. Her youngest child, a little girl of three, stood at the window with her and held her hand.

The October evening was brilliant and cool. Philip should have enjoyed the drive from Alcala, especially perhaps the last few miles, through lands to which her husband's care had brought so much contentment. He had always cherished the humaneness of Ruy Gomez, and Ana had sometimes heard him muse enviously on what he called the latter's "curiously practical application of goodwill to life". She had teased him then about his adverb "curiously", pointing out that his own goodwill often took practical shape. And he had said that it pleased him to hear that from her, who was "no courtier". "No courtier, sir; only a subject who admires her king."

How long since she had said that to him? Seven, eight years ago? At least; because she had said it in the queen's presence. She remembered Isabel de Valois' soft, appreciative smile—and it was eight years now since that lovely creature's death. If she were alive still and on the throne, instead of this dull poor girl from Austria—why she would be thirty, incredible as it seemed. And perhaps even beginning to look something like a match for her middle-aged husband.

Ana, thirty-six herself, smiled on the word 'middle-aged', and let her glance pass over the market-place to the roof of the Colegiata church, where her husband slept, with round him

I

the small bones of four of their ten children. Life was moving on indeed. They were dim now, the vivid, hopeful days when she and the princess from France were brides together. Spain had seemed impregnable then, the king was gay and self-confident, and the tragedy of Don Carlos had not advanced its shadow very far. Now there were many graves; much blundering, war and trouble; the king worked like a mole, people said, and court life appeared to have degenerated into a cryptic, stuffy routine, directed by a few fanatical canons from Sevilla, and some upstart clerks from no one knew where.

Ana had not visited Madrid or opened her house there since her husband's death. Nothing tempted her thither, and she had learnt to love, with a constancy which sometimes amused her, the exhalation of bright peace which rose to her morning, noon and evening from this landscape of Pastrana, which was both her home and her charge. It was indeed an oasis in the proud poverty of Castile.

And she, very Castilian, had mocked the first efforts to make it so.

"You Portuguese peasant," she used to say to her husband, "would you mind telling me why two blades of grass are so certainly better than one?"

But Ruy insisted that to starve was not essential to Castilian character, and pointed out to her that she had grown into a very true example of her own race on a lifetime of good meals.

So the land which Philip gave them had been irrigated, manured and planted. A colony of persecuted 'Moriscos' had been immigrated from Valencia and established in Pastrana, to teach the people their good farming methods, and in particular how to cultivate the mulberry tree and make silk. Here they and their children still were, happy, tolerant and tolerated. Pastrana was prosperous.

This was a commendable state of affairs, and sufficiently

remarkable in a Castilian village; and although Ana had jibed in her time at its bringing about, yet now that Ruy, the good landlord, was dead and that his king's new policies were making waste of his statesman-like work for Spain, she thought with pleasure sometimes that here at least in his own village the first Duke of Pastrana would be remembered for a generation or two as a man of goodwill.

Philip might be thinking similar thoughts as he drove past the stripped mulberry farms and the weavers' sheds. For the king was a faithful friend. She knew better than most how faithful. And knowing, wondered now what especial whim of avuncular fuss brought him all this way to-day to visit her. True, his happening to be the guest, near-by at Alcala, of the Marqués de los Velez, would appear to the court to minimise the great honour done to Ruy Gomez's widow—and Philip would undoubtedly think of that, for no one was more careful of appearances. Nevertheless, busy and tired as he was, to make this journey and risk the gossip of Madrid, meant that some aspect of her affairs must now have been worrying him for many months. For on principle he never examined any anxiety when it first arose to him. But having always held himself as, after Ruy, the guardian of her and her children, he kept informed about her, and during the early months of her widowhood had written her many fussy letters about this and that. And Ana, being herself incapable of fuss and unsympathetic to it, yet marvelled, as she read these letters, at his kind-heartedness, and his gusto for detail. She had once observed to Ruy that surely this latter peculiarity of Philip's must be ultimately destructive to him as a king, but they had agreed that it made him oddly endearing as a man and a companion.

It would be pleasant to Ana, even stimulating, to see Philip again after so long a time. His admiration of her was constant, and had always pleased her. Thinking of that, she glanced back over her shoulder towards the bad Dutch portrait of her husband which hung in the room. In the flat, conventional painting she could find no hint of the urbane grace and friendliness of the man who had so surprisingly commanded her life in thirteen years. She sighed a little and cupped her fingers over the black silk patch that covered her right eye. She reflected that, in regard to his marriage, Ruy had lived exactly long enough for the completion of his own devoted purpose—which had simply been, she used to tell him, to train her out of being herself. He had known, it seemed, when to dismiss himself, known exactly how much imposition of time and habit was needed to lacquer a wild heart.

Yes, you sleep in peace, she mused ironically to the portrait now, you sleep in peace because you know your *Tuerta* is growing old, and soon will be quite old, a very old woman in charge of a very tidy parish. You kept me safe, Ruy—you insisted on that—and now you know that even a King of Spain can do nothing against the attrition of the years——

Ana de Mendoza y de la Cerda, Princess of Eboli and Duchess of Pastrana, was the only child of the Prince of Mélito, and therefore heiress in her own right to the estates, privileges and titles of one of the greatest lines of the house of Mendoza, the leading family of Spain. This family, Viscayan in origin and now holding lands all over the peninsula, had nevertheless, at the time of Ana's birth in 1540, been Castilian in root and spirit for over three hundred years.

She was physically the expression of what that implied. Her beauty, for those who found her beautiful, was, paradoxically, of exaggeration and restraint. She was taller and thinner than is averagely considered seductive in a woman; her bones were narrow, and every feature, nose, chin, hand and foot, was a little longer than it should be. Her skin was thinly white, with blue veins showing on her temples and her hands. Her left eye was full of light, but over the socket of the right one she wore, as has been said, a black silk eye-shade, cut in diamond shape. She had worn this since she was fourteen. At that age she fought a duel with a page in her father's house, and lost her right eye.

So when Ruy Gomez de Silva returned from England and Flanders in 1559 to consummate the marriage which he had contracted six years before with the child-heiress of the Mendozas, he found her *tuerta*, one-eyed.

She made no drama of this. Her husband and her mother were allowed to call her *Tuerta*, as a caress, in private; but she preferred the disfigurement ignored as a rule, and no one had ever heard that it troubled her. She seemed to wear her black silk patch as naturally as her shoes.

Her husband had always thought her extraordinarily beautiful, and had understood well that many men envied him and thought his luck fantastic. For he was forty-two and she was nineteen when they first slept together, and yet the fourteen years of married life which he enjoyed with her had been warm and happy, in spite of a courtier-world which did not spare them spatterings of dishonour.

For Ana was not merely too rich and important to escape slander. She was, even under Ruy's guardianship, too careless. Also her husband was the king's favourite minister of state and, all through his life, was given every privilege and kindness in Philip's power. Therefore Madrid said again and again that Ana was the king's mistress, and by her husband's will. And Ana often smiled at the awkward perspicacity of gossips, who will often locate accurately enough what they might call a situation, but can seldom manage to interpret its truth.

But now she was forgotten by the chatterers of Madrid. And Philip, the once-handsome and scandal-giving king, was an over-worked and over-worried middle-aged man, concerned to breed a male heir who might be hoped to grow to manhood, and otherwise tortured by the repercussions from his own obstinate conception of kingship.

Such news as Ana heard in these days, from visiting relations, or from the echoes of Alcala University, picked up by her son Rodrigo, made it seem that Spain was facing grave trouble, at home and abroad. But what seemed to her most alarming was that no one, none of the great princes or captains of her own family, for instance, either knew or desired to know exactly what those troubles were, or how they could be met or avoided. Spanish policy was the king's business now, apparently. And all that was asked of the nobility was that it should live ostentatiously, practise its religion, marry and breed.

It was Philip's wily foreign father, Ana knew, who had so carefully altered the principle of Castilian government. After his defeat of the *Comuneros* he had directed himself to making absolute the power of the Spanish monarchy. And he had succeeded curiously well.

In her husband's lifetime Ana had often fretted to him disgustedly about the growing indolence and indifference of the Spanish nobility before the general question of Spanish destiny. Old lords and vassal-holders lived lazily on their estates and gossiped detachedly about the foreign wars and the religious troubles abroad; their sons commanded the king's regiments or ships as directed, and without caring why they did so—or they sailed for adventure to the western empire, to make fortunes, or they joined the Church, or they played the fool expensively in Madrid, and made fun of the vulgar new politicians who manœuvred portentously round the self-important and over-pious king.

But Ruy, a 'vulgar, new politician' himself, an 'upstart from Portugal', laughed at her, and said that it would do Spain no harm to have a rest from the *pundonor*, egotism and all-round posturing nonsense of the Castilian lords, and that Charles and Philip were men of executive power, good cosmopolitans, of whom the country had great need.

Provided the king's ministers were chosen well, this new method of government by Cabinet was safe, he thought, and assuredly worth trying for one or two generations. For Ruy believed in change, and in getting things done. But Ana, the Castilian, laughed at him and said that time often showed the great advantage of *not* getting things done, and that anyway ancient rights were ancient rights. To this her husband retorted that no one had withdrawn the ancient rights of Castile, and that if they *were* falling into disuse, was that any reason why Philip II should not proceed with the government of Spain?

But such talk belonged to the days when she had been near the throne and had inside news of great events. Now she was an obscure country widow, concerned with olive harvests, sheep-shearings and silkworms—and perhaps with her children too, she thought with a little laugh, looking down at the silky head of her baby daughter.

The *Colegiata* bells began to peal. The chimes of the convents took up the message, and lastly, the Town Hall bell threw in its pompous weight. A hum of pleasure rose from the crowd in the market-place. The little girl tugged at her mother's hand, and Ana picked her up and went on to the balcony with her for a moment.

"Yes, he's coming now, Anichu! The king they've been so boastful about!"

All the de Silva children except this baby Ana had met the king, though Fernando, who was only six now, could not really remember his one encounter with Philip II, which had taken place before he was two. But the four boys often teased the baby with this superiority of theirs, even making her cry. So to-day she was eager to catch up with them, and meet the king.

The buzz in the town soon became a cheer, and then a spreading and at last united cry of welcome. Ana could see the first horsemen coming up the street towards the market-place. She admired the easy way the people parted into a lane for the cavalcade. The cheers were warm but measured; they sounded a full welcome, but they were also contained within a border of etiquette. They suggested that Philip was immeasurably welcome to their town, but that they understood that he was here on private business and had no desire to force a state occasion on him. Ruy would have approved these cheers, she thought.

As the hoofs and wheels rattled into the market-place, Ana withdrew from the balcony and walked across the room to a chair near the chimney-piece. She set her protesting little daughter on a stool beside her, and laughed at her indignation.

"No, Anichu, we simply can't peep at him from overhead; that isn't etiquette, and Rodrigo would be furious!"

The clatter was in the forecourt now, and she could hear the king's carriage drawing up before the door. Poor little vain Rodrigo! She hoped nothing would go wrong with his beautifully polished speech of welcome. He was beginning on it now perhaps, with his three pretty brothers standing behind him—all nicer boys than he, in their mother's private opinion. Don Francisco, the chaplain, was ready with his speech too. And no doubt her secretary would get himself presented. And as many of the children's tutors as dared. But it was all worked out to a nicety, of course; Rodrigo would leave nothing to chance! And how delighted he had been when she had said that she would not be present in the hall for the king's arrival, but would leave him to do the honours, as second Duke of Pastrana. This was the kind of liberty that she could always take with Philip—and she hated official occasions. Besides, whatever Rodrigo thought, it was not to him, young peacock, that she was really entrusting the reception downstairs, but to her butler, Diego, whose poise was such that Ruy used to say at five minutes' notice he could have taken up office as *mayordomo* of El Escorial. And

Bernardina, her *dueña*, would take everything in very shrewdly, and report it all to her for her amusement afterwards.

But then, impulsively, and not, as Rodrigo would believe, with intention to exasperate or humiliate him, Ana overthrew the ordained plan of the king's reception, and picking up her baby daughter, ran down the stairs to welcome him herself. For as she sat in the upper room she realised that she was very glad indeed that he had come to see her and it occurred to her that he would be disappointed not to find her waiting for him with her sons. So she ran very quickly round the galleried corridor, and paused for a second at the top of the staircase, before descending into the patio.

"You mustn't giggle when you meet the king," she whispered to her delighted little daughter.

She could hear Rodrigo's clear, pretty voice fluting gracefully through his speech.

" . . . and also, Sire, on behalf of my mother, Her Highness the Princess of Eboli, who did not wish your first moments here, after travel, to be overtaxed with ceremony, and will be most happy to make her own obeisance of welcome and duty to Your Majesty at whatever later hour of this evening which it may please Your Majesty to appoint . . ."

Ana had half-descended the staircase now, unnoticed by anyone save Bernardina, and the king. The latter's eyes, having found her, stayed upon her as she moved quickly round the group of welcomers and dropped on her knees between him and her astonished, speeching son. She placed her baby daughter also on her knees.

"Bend your head a little, Anichu," she said softly, and then looked up and smiled at Philip as she took and kissed his outstretched hand.

"Your Majesty is most warmly welcome to this honoured house, and all that it contains is naturally yours and at your absolute service."

Philip smiled at her slowly and she rose as he drew up his hand.

"Thank you, Princess. It gives me pleasure to see you again, and your family and your people. Is this the little one, the last?"

He put his hand on the baby girl's head.

"Yes, Your Majesty. This is Ana de Silva, Your Majesty's most obedient and honoured servant."

The Princess stood aside then, on the king's left, and allowed her little sons and the other members of the household to make their bows and murmur their loyalty. But there were no more set speeches, not even Rodrigo's peroration. Instead the welcome came to life, and the king thanked them all for being so glad to see him, and laughed when Fernando, aged six, politely ventured to correct his assumption that this was their first meeting.

"Princess, I do not think that you know my Secretary of State? May I present Don Mateo Vasquez—Doña Ana de Silva y de Mendoza, Princess of Eboli."

The tall dark priest who stood behind the king came forward and bowed. Ana looked at him shrewdly as she returned his salutation. She had heard of him. He had taken unimportant office at the Court a year before her husband's death, but within the last twelve months his favour as a counsellor was said to have risen very high with the king. He belonged, Ana understood, to that party, or *amistad*, at court which her husband had led in his lifetime, and which stood for progressiveness at home, and tolerance and non-violence abroad. But she thought now that he did not look like a man of tolerance.

Mateo Vasquez was somewhat stiff in his movements.

"His Majesty does me a very great honour, Your Highness, in bringing me to your illustrious house." Ana thought that even Rodrigo would think this etiquette heavy. "I had the privilege to be in some measure acquainted with Your

Highness's late illustrious husband, His Highness the Prince of Eboli, whom we all still mourn as one of Spain's greatest servants."

The Princess of Eboli did not like the Andalusian accent.

"He's very likely a Moor," she thought flippantly. "What on earth's come over Philip?" And hardly troubling to hide boredom, she turned from the still speechifying Secretary of State, to greet Fray Diego de Chaves, the King's chaplain.

And now the doors of the house chapel stood open, and the whole group moved towards them, to offer the customary word of thanksgiving to God that his Majesty had once more enjoyed safe transit from one place to another.

Ana walked to the chapel by the king's side.

"I miss Ruy very much even now, Ana," he said to her. "Often when I'm overtired, I forget he's gone, and look forward to his counsel—and then——"

"I miss him too," she said.

Rodrigo offered the king holy water in a silver bowl. The king dipped his fingers and spoke once more to his hostess before he crossed the threshold.

"Last time I was in this chapel, it was to see Mother Teresa herself give the Discalced habit to two of her Pastrana novices." Philip said this very softly, and with a curious half-smile. But Ana winced. She did not like to be reminded of Mother Teresa.

"And now perhaps Your Majesty will pray for any so unlucky as to be disliked by that great woman."

The king smiled more broadly.

"They say that she's a saint, Ana."

"I have always thought so, Your Majesty," Ana whispered back, but the dropped voice did not relax its mockery.

"Te Deum laudamus . . ." Fray Diego was chanting.

Philip suppressed his smile and made the sign of the Cross as he entered the chapel.

## II

An hour later one of the king's pages came to Ana's drawing-room. He said that His Majesty was taking a *merienda*, a light refreshment, in his own apartments, and, that consumed, he desired to give himself the pleasure of talking to Her Highness. He would like to come to this drawing-room, if that was agreeable to Her Highness?

It was agreeable.

It was dark outside now, so Ana had the great window shut and the curtains drawn. The fire was burning well, but the servants piled it still higher with logs and pine-cones; they lighted candles, and withdrew.

Ana was not quite sure if she liked her most recent re-decoration of this beautiful room. She had had it done early in the year under the influence of an access of gaiety and excitement, which she had half-thought she might express in a brief return to social life, by giving a house-party at Easter, or a banquet for Rodrigo's birthday, or—or something. That had been her mood then, restless, extravagant, but un-directed. But during Lent her mother, the Princess of Mélito, had died, and mourning shrouded the house. There was no party to justify the new paints and tapestries, which she imagined Philip would not care for. He had been fond of the room in its more austere days of plain white walls and dark red hangings, and would be bound to resent as too experimental this all-over design of gold acacia-leaves painted on white. Probably he would be right. But the heavy plain gold silk of the curtains was a triumph of the Pastrana looms, and so was the dark green velvet of the chairs and cushions. And the pictures were mostly favourites of the king's: a Giorgione landscape that always led him on to talk of Titian; a Clouet head of a boy that Isabel of Valois had given her; her own dark, sober portrait by Sanchez Coëllo; a Holbein

drawing of a woman's head which Ruy had sent to her from
England twenty years ago; Ruy's portrait, which Philip
admired, by the Dutchman Antonio Moro; and, hung in a
bad light, so as not to annoy her too much, a gift from the
king, a "St. Peter Weeping" by Pantoja de la Cruz—a
picture which bored Ana extremely.

To-night, however, whether or not Philip would approve
of it, the room in which she awaited him pleased her by its
lighted-up, expectant air. Returning to it from her bedroom
now, and pausing on the threshold, she noticed this and her
own irrational response of pleasure.

Anyone would think that something momentous was in the
air, she thought, whereas actually I am only going to be
bored by some wild-cat match-making scheme for one of the
children, or a legal catch in Mother's will, or Heaven knows
what! Still, she felt exhilarated by the room's beauty.

There were roses on an Italian table near the fire. They
looked very beautiful there, but she wondered if they would
get too hot and die quickly. However, as she stood and
considered where else to place them, the great door at the
north end of the room opened, and the king was announced
and came towards her.

She dropped on her knees before him again, and by the
time she rose the door was shut and they were alone.

He looked about him appraisingly.

"You didn't tell me you were making all these changes."

"Are your subjects really to worry you about their new
wall-paint and cushion-covers?"

"I think I like it, Ana. Surprising and—worldly, for a
country house. But—it suits you."

He gave her his slow smile, and sat down near the fire.
Ana went and sat at the other side of the hearth.

"It's a long time since I have felt worldly," she said.

"Just as well for your immortal soul, I suppose."

"Your interest in the soul increases," she said demurely.

"It's an interest you were once inclined to force on me, Ana."

"I, Your Majesty?"

He laughed outright. When they were alone she used formality of address only to get effects of irony or innocence. The device amused him.

"Your virtue was a silent sermon to me on the importance of the soul. Indeed, Ana, it was a succession of sermons."

She heard him with a certain confusion which was novel to her. For this surely, memory said, was Philip in sensual mood, Philip riding up to the imperious question of his desire. And Ana had for years now regarded that Philip as a ghost, a departed lover, unsatisfied but appeased, the memory of whose subdued passion gave a peculiar interest and character to her relationship with the man who stood in his place, Philip the king, the family friend. However, she answered him as she thought best and kindest.

"Your affection for Ruy was your true censor, Philip. And as for my 'virtue'—I should hate to think that it preached 'silent sermons' anywhere, to anyone!"

The king had been pleased by the first part of her speech, but now he looked disturbed. He did not wish anything that he had ever desired to be made to seem cheap of access.

"I, for one, have always believed in it in any case—no matter what Madrid had to say about you, Ana."

She laughed at him.

"So well you might, Philip. Considering that Madrid's only charge against me was that I slept with the king!"

He looked a little startled.

"I had forgotten your free way of speech, my dear!"

"I'm sorry—does it annoy you now?"

He half-stretched out a hand towards her, and she, without taking it, noticed the ageing, thickened texture of its skin.

"On the contrary. It reminds me of good days—and it does suggest, Heaven forgive you! that death is not on the doorstep yet."

"You and old Death! What a surprise you'd get if he forgot you, Philip!"

"Forgot me?"

"Is it *lèse-majesté* to suggest it?"

Philip was sitting upright in his chair, his elbows on the arms of it, his hands clasped loosely together. He looked brighter of eye, more invigorated than when he had entered the room, Ana thought. And as he leant towards her, shaking his head in mock reproval of her flippancy, he was conscious of freshness and gaiety within himself. He recognised the sensation as her particular gift to him; always with her it had been like this. Always, sitting with Ana, he had felt confidence in himself, he had felt warmed and well. But he must resist this unsuitable comfort now—or at least resist awareness of it. It might introduce, or reveal, disingenuousness in him for the business about to be discussed.

"Your audacity has always amused me, and been permitted—as you know well, Ana," he said, "but I have travelled here in order to talk of serious matters."

"I know—it is extraordinarily kind of you. What are these serious matters, Your Majesty?"

He dismissed the mock-innocence of the query with a flick of his hand.

"You must return to Madrid, and take hold of your complicated family affairs."

Ana paused before she made an answer. This was a curious command from Philip. Hardly a year ago, when her father had pleaded with the king to make her return to Madrid for reasons of family convenience, he had deliberately refrained, and had reminded the Prince of Mélito of her husband's desire that she should live as much as possible at Pastrana, away from the troubles of the Court and her much ramified family.

"Has Father been getting at you, for some dark reason?"

"No. The Prince of Mélito isn't worrying about his daughter at present. He's preoccupied——"

He smiled, but Ana's face was contemptuous.

"So I hear.  Courting Magdalena de Aragon, isn't he?"

The king nodded.

"And mother hardly cold!  Disgusting old fool!"

"Ana!  He *is* your father, and a great prince.  He wants a male heir, and, after all, he still has time to get one."  This was said with faint mischief, as Ana took free and full enjoyment always from her position as a great heiress in her own right.

"Still has time?  He can't be much off seventy."

"Sixty-five, perhaps."

"Well then?"

"Five years older than Ruy would be, if he were still alive, Ana."

She laughed away the surprise of that.

"If that's true it makes no difference.  Ruy was a man—and he managed to get the heirs he wanted in suitable time.  Poor Magdalena!  Will they really marry her off to father?"

"They'll be foolish if they don't," said Philip.  "And indirectly it *is* this intention of your father's that brings me here.  But primarily—have you heard that since your mother is dead without producing male issue, your cousin, Iñigo Lopez de Mendoza, is taking legal opinion on whether he has not an equal claim with you to the Mélito inheritance—since you are a woman."

Ana sat up very straight.

"What madness!" she said.

"Actually, no.  It appears to be quite a point."

"Salic law—in Castile?"

Philip laughed.

"Well, a whiff of it here and there in some of our families!"

"How barbarous!  Does Iñigo really think he has a case?"

"More importantly, certain lawyers think he has.  But you

see, Ana, *if* he has, *and* if your father marries again and gets a male heir——"

She laughed merrily.

"Ah then! What a sad waste of my cousin's perspicacity!"

Philip shook his head at her.

"Not necessarily. If Iñigo does establish an equal claim with you to the Mendoza estates, a part of that claim might stand, I think, no matter how well Magdalena does her duty. As you will not lose everything by the birth of a brother, it appears to me that Iñigo, once roused, will stick to his claim on your claim——"

"So I am threatened with ruin whatever happens!" She threw up her hands in mock horror—for she did not really believe in these threats to her established splendour, and also she was not mercenary or easily alarmed about material things. "Here I sit ruined and Your Majesty's mysterious command to me is to go to Madrid at once, and ruin myself entirely!"

"Not quite that. I desire you to do what Ruy would think necessary in the situation as it is."

Ana's one eye looked straight into the king's grave face. Her voice betrayed no humour and no reserves of meaning when she spoke.

"In the situation as I think it may be, Philip—I know very well what Ruy would insist on."

Philip raised his brows. He seemed suspicious, as if he felt truth probing a little under their serenity.

"Yes, Ana?"

"He would insist on locking me up, in the hour of battle! He always said it was the only thing to do—don't you remember?" She leant her head against the tall back of her chair and laughed in reminiscence. " 'I like my quarrels moderated,' he would say, 'so we'll just keep Ana out of it!' "

Philip felt a pang of irritation.

"He knew you."

"No, Philip. The point was that he knew he didn't know me."

The king smiled.

"Women like to say vainglorious things."

"No doubt. But I don't speak vaingloriously now."

Her gaze was on the fire, her profile towards Philip; but before she spoke again she cupped the fingers of her right hand over her black eye-shade, so that her face was hooded from him. He could only observe the exaggerated beauty of her fingers.

"Ruy would know that," she went on, speaking softly and slowly. "It is *true* that we didn't know each other very well— though we did get each other's meanings when we talked!"

Philip shrank, offended as perhaps she meant him to be.

"By his own wit and skill," she went on, "he evolved for himself a far better wife than I am a woman! The wife he wanted, in fact—and it wasn't me. Wasn't that clever of him, Philip? Didn't he deserve to be your Secretary of State?"

Philip did not respond to her sudden gay turn towards him, for her voice and the strain of her reminiscence offended him. He thought she showed poor taste in compelling him to eavesdrop on her enigmatic sentimentality. He had loved his servant Ruy Gomez, and could praise him richly in the right place—but the least of his love had been given to him as Ana's husband.

"I tried to reward him according to his high deserts," he said primly, "but I have always known that in arranging his marriage with you I excelled myself."

"Dear Philip! Forgive me for boring you. And be so good as to tell me why you command me to return to Madrid."

She evoked with pleasure the king's reassured response to the word "command", which, for her own part, she had enjoyed using. When, in private, she called him "Sire" and "Majesty", she knew that the irony she put into such phrases never fell quite easily on Philip's sensitive ears. He enjoyed her feminine impudence in playing with them, enjoyed the hint of *liaison*, but also suspected that in doing so His Most Catholic Majesty lapsed, that the man almost winked at the symbol. On the other hand when suddenly, with immaculate and simple intonation, as conventionally in fact as if writing to him, this arrogant princess professed obedience, or asked for his commands, he was profoundly pleased. He felt more kingly then; it was as if Ana de Mendoza's acknowledgment reconsecrated him, from time to time, upon his throne.

She knew this foible, and liked to pander to it. The absurdity brightened her own pride, for although, as the greatest lady in Spain, she had an immense self-confidence, inborn from centuries of authority, and although she therefore regarded the uneasy son of Charles V as *parvenu* in the Peninsula, she had histrionic moods, and it pleased her sometimes to observe how a selected word or intonation of hers might reassure the King of Spain.

"There are a number of reasons, Ana. This probable lawsuit is only one—but it will necessitate prolonged stays in Madrid when it develops. The marriage arrangements of your father——" She made an impatient movement—"it will be necessary for us to study the legal position well, in order that the Duke of Segorbe does not swindle your children on behalf of his daughter——"

"But I am only forty miles from Madrid here, Philip! Can't these things be dealt with as other business matters are?"

"No, Ana—because, as your guardian, I must give thought and consultation to your affairs—and I dislike infrequent conferences and hasty decisions——"

Ana smiled. If Philip truly proposed to interest himself in whatever division of her estates lay ahead, then indeed there would be "thought and consultation". Nevertheless she suspected somewhat the motives underlying this anxiety.

"Naturally," she murmured, keeping her tone noncommittal.

"But there are other reasons why you must restore your associations with Madrid," he went on, rather more irritably. "I feel it my duty to keep a closer eye than I have been doing upon the education of Ruy's sons, and therefore I desire to have the children, for some parts of the year at least, where they may come under my observation. And, now that Rodrigo has been elected a page, and has duties to fulfil at Court——"

"He was happy and well looked-after when he was on duty at the Escorial in August——"

"Yes. But during a part of the winter he will have to be at Court in Madrid—and I think that he should live in your house then, Ana. He seems to be a rather vain and self-centred boy—a mother's influence——"

Ana laughed. She was not at all maternal. Towards her children she behaved as towards other acquaintances or dependants, occupying herself with those whom she liked, more or less ignoring the others. Rodrigo bored her.

"A mother's influence. Rodrigo knows nothing about that, Philip. And I promise you that boy will live as he will live!"

"As you know, I disapprove of your parental theories, Ana—that is why I must have the children nearer to me."

"I can't resist pointing out to you," she answered, "that if the gossips of Madrid heard the tone in which you say that, they'd surely revive some old stories, Philip!"

He glanced at her with sharp pleasure, which he tried to conceal.

"The gossips of Madrid! They are my final reason for wanting you to come out of hiding."

"Why—are they running short of scandal-matter?"

"On the contrary. Be serious, Ana. You are the bearer of a great family tradition, you have duties which could be called impersonal, I think. Well, one of those duties is to live in the light, as the daughter and the mother of great Spanish houses."

"I did that, and it wasn't liked."

The king chuckled.

"Neither is the other thing, dear child."

"Why—what on earth?" She was truly puzzled.

"They are saying things about you, Ana, that we cannot have said."

"For instance?"

"Well——" he laughed and looked at her with deep gentleness, to remove hurt from his words, "one story is that, since Ruy's death, you have lost your wits, that you are mad. Another is that you are a miser, and ill-treat your family and servants. Some even say—I believe—that you are dead, Ana. That I had you killed, for some strange reason." He paused and stared into the fire.

She guessed that he was thinking of Isabel of Valois, and of his dead son, Carlos.

She stretched forward and touched his hand lightly in compassion.

"Philip! Philip! Do you still care about the things they say?"

He did not answer her. His eyes had a cold, hurt look as he stared into the past—or perhaps into the future, for Ana imagined that he might well be haranguing posterity at that moment, insisting to it that he was virtuous, both as man and king.

She leant back in her chair again, and considered him. She found him interesting in this interview, as always at past meetings she had done.

Ana had never travelled outside Spain, indeed outside Castile, but from childhood and afterwards, until her husband's death, she had been accustomed to meet the most distinguished Spaniards of the time, and such celebrated foreigners as came to the Spanish Court. But very few of

these made even a passing impression, and none, unrelated
to her, was even dimly remembered once he passed. Save
this one man—Philip, the king.

She had met him first when she was a child, eleven years
old. She often rode with her father in the Retiro Wood
outside Madrid, which was then only a little town made
fashionable by the Emperor's idea that its climate was good
for his health. Philip, the prince, rode there too sometimes,
and once or twice reined in his horse to talk with the Count of
Mélito. He was accompanied, whenever she saw him, by the
same thin, dark, gracious little man, Ruy Gomez de Silva,
whom her father professed to dislike, but whom he always
greeted, the child observed, with particular cordiality.
Listening to these brief, complimentary exchanges in which,
naturally, she was not expected to participate, Ana liked to
hear the informal foreign wit break against her father's dry
Castilian ironies. It was like the play of sunny waves on a
rock, and it surprised her that anything Portuguese could be
so graceful.

But it was the prince himself who held her eyes. To the
eleven-year-old girl a man of twenty-four who was already a
father and a widower should be old, and out of any kind of
sympathetic reach, but this Philip—let them talk as they
willed of his cares and burdens—was simply a boy on a pony.
He was practically a contemporary, she decided, and were he
not heir to the throne, she could have spoken with him as
with her cousins at Guadalajara or Toledo. More happily,
perhaps, since she found him more attractive than they.

His eyes were blue, and his hair was very fair. He was the
first fair-haired person Ana had ever seen. His badly under-
hung jaw—about which, as about his father's, she had often
heard her relatives sneer—did in fact shock her at first sight
by its brutality of line; but it also gave to his face a sulkiness
and reserve with which she sympathised, and which increased
her impression, at each interview, that he and she were

young, and thus divided from the other two, who were indisputably grown up.

Philip had laughed delightedly in later years at this account of the impression he made on a little girl in the Retiro Wood in 1551. It seemed that he, for his part, had hardly been aware of her presence at those encounters; in his mind she had not been a person then, but rather a very important counter in his complicated scheme of rewards and promotions. She was matrimonially the greatest prize in Spain, and he had wanted her reserved for his faithful friend, Ruy Gomez. That had been the chief motive, he told her, of the cordial gossips with her father.

In return for this confession of Philip's, Ana did not ever tell him—lest he should use it to hurt Ruy—that when in her thirteenth year she began to pick up inaccurately some wisps of gossip floating round her father's house—about her future destiny, and the vastness of the arrangements to be made for it; when she heard the prince's name crop up again and again in dark talk of settlements; when servants winked, and *dueñas* and tutors gossiped unctuously of royal favour and royal presents—she decided, alone and without asking questions—that she had been chosen to be Philip's second wife. It had seemed to her a very good idea. She knew enough history and was sufficiently a bigoted Castilian to believe that nothing could better enhance Philip's moral and temporal rights in the Peninsula than marriage with a Mendoza. She also knew that, by reason of her birth, she would marry by arrangement and as family interests directed —so she thought it lucky that these interests should ally her with a fair-haired boy instead of with a staid and bearded grandee from Andalusia or Santander, such as had carried off some of her girl-cousins. And dreaming with a forthrightness always to be characteristic of her, she braced herself with inward pleasure towards the difficult proposition of being Queen of Spain. But nobody ever knew that the little girl was both surprised and bored when she discovered that she was only asked to be the wife of His Majesty's favourite Secretary of State.

In June 1552 Ana celebrated her twelfth birthday. Before Christmas of that year her mother told her of the marriage that was being arranged for her. In April its settlements were signed in Madrid, and a few days afterwards, in the chapel of her father's house at Alcala de Henares, the little girl, not yet thirteen, was married to the thirty-six-year-old Secretary of State.

Prince Philip drove from El Pardo to be present at the ceremony and do honour to his friend, Ruy Gomez. He told Ana later in life that it was always his impression that he had never seen her before that day.

The marriage contract was a mighty transaction, almost a minor treaty. It was at once formal, shrewd and sacramental, as every major act of a Mendoza had to be; but also it was legendarily suggestive of worldly promise, since the bride-groom was the most gifted and honoured statesman in Philip's train. It was heavy with endowments, scattering money, lands and titles like roses on its two participants; it fulfilled so many of the Prince of Mélito's petulant ambitions that he could almost forget his son-in-law was an upstart whose Portuguese grandfather had been a nobody in the train of the Infanta Isabel. And its trend was so correct, in that it set its true, enormous price on pure Castilian blood, that the bride's father was enabled to look indulgently upon one clause of it which, for being novel, appeared to him faintly offensive—the clause which secured that this marriage should not be consummated until two years after the date of its formal enactment. A new-fangled and unnecessary idea, Don Diego thought, as he let it pass.

But the bridegroom waited more than six years for his consummation. At sunset on his wedding day, the wines drunk and the Benediction sung, he bade farewell to Ana, and departed with Philip to El Pardo, there to plunge as eagerly as ever into that cabinet-work on foreign affairs to which both gave unresting zeal. Naples, France, the Papacy, the Sultan Soliman—in talk of all these they may well have forgotten as they drove upwards through the pinewoods that the day had begun with a wedding. And soon there was all the work of arranging for Philip to marry Mary of England. The two departed in due time—to England and the Netherlands. When they returned Ana was a tall young woman in her twentieth year, who wore a diamond-shaped black patch over the cavity of her right eye; Ruy, grown somewhat grey about the temples, had won a European reputation in diplomacy and was more than ever Philip's favourite minister; and Philip himself was King of Spain, and once again a widower.

At the time of Ruy's marriage to Ana, Philip had conferred on him the principality of Eboli, with estates in the Kingdom of Naples. Ana always mocked at this Italian title. In Spain there were no princes outside the royal house, and it seemed to her ridiculous that for instance her uncle, the Duke of Infantado, should have to debate precedence with her father, whose new title of Prince of Mélito was Italian and therefore, in her view, an absurd encumbrance for a Spaniard. Shortly after his marriage Ruy had purchased the neglected estates of Pastrana from Ana's father; he established his family there and used the village experimentally for the application of his theories of agrarian and social reform. In the success of the experiment and in the increasing love for each other which he and Ana found there, they grew to love the place. And the king, pleased with all that they did for their people, created the new dukedom of Pastrana and added it to their honours. To Ana's very Spanish satisfaction. This native title conferred, she dissuaded Ruy from handing on the Neapolitan principality to his heir, coaxed him to get rid of his Italian estates, and prevailed upon him to found their house simply as the dukedom of Pastrana. Yet throughout her own life-time she had to bear as good-humouredly as she could the appellation of Princess of Eboli—a foreign vulgarity at which she never ceased to jibe.

However, Philip's showy open-handedness with honours carried brilliance and power and even gaiety with it in the early days of his reign. And Ana was designed to embellish these. So she advanced into her married life in brilliant appetite for all that it chanced to offer.

She found inspiriting company about the king.

Isabel of Valois came from Paris to marry Philip in 1560, and when Ana first surveyed her, in the Infantado palace in Guadalajara, she smiled in gay suspicion upon Ruy, who a few months before had had to leave their bridal bed to go and do Philip's wooing of this girl in France. But, "No, Ana," he told her. "It was her fat, intelligent mother I had to dally with." Isabel was fifteen then—the same age as Philip's son, Carlos, for whom indeed, while Mary Tudor lived, she had been docketed. But throughout the royal wedding ceremony, whatever cynical Castilians and watchful ambassadors may have been thinking, and however much the unhappily tempered young heir apparent may or may not have been raging in his dark heart against his father, Ana de Mendoza at least, taking her high part in all the ritual, believed quite simply that the beautiful foreign girl was lucky in the accident that gave her to the King of Spain.

Yet she had not the luck to live. And she was unlucky, unkind to Philip, Ana thought, in that she died in the same dark year with Carlos. Ruy said that 1568 made the king into an old and frightened man—and, as usual, Ruy was right. Those two young deaths and all the evil stories which arose from them had made Philip understand that even the divine right is not a sufficient armour for a king. Yet armour he must have—justification; he must not only be correct in his every action but the world must see his rectitude. And since

two such premisses to peace were impossible, he grew
increasingly frightened.

As Ana considered all this and related it to the expression of
uneasy sullenness on the king's face now, compassion cooled
in her and she recalled another observation of her husband's—
that a man as diseasedly frightened as Philip and possessed of
so much power could be very frightening to others.

I have never been afraid of him, she thought. He is cruel;
not simply cruel as his half-barbarous old father could be, and
not madly so, like Carlos. But cruel with piety, cruel in self-
justification, cruel because a king must be right. I have never
been afraid of all that. I have sometimes thought it graceless,
sometimes stupid—and sometimes, for all I know or care, it
may have been justifiable. But cruelty drops from him when
he feels safe. He was never cruel to Isabel, nor is he to his
other wife, who worships him. He is never cruel to his
children, or to the very poor or the very weak. Or to his real
friends, like Ruy. And he has never been anything but kind
to me. He feels very safe with me. But if he were *not* to feel
safe? And what does he really want of me now?

"Why do they think that you have had me killed, Philip?"

He came back slowly from his debate with posterity,
sighed a little and then smiled at her.

"Perhaps they think I'd like an old scandal tidied up! I
have such a mania for order."

"You talk as if we *had* a guilty secret!"

"Sometimes I'm a little sorry that we haven't, Ana!"

She knew now what he half-intended and half-dreaded in
this appeal to her to return to Madrid and the Court. He was
playing with an impulse he neither believed in nor approved
of, but which would never set him entirely free—since, as he
was King of Spain, it was impossible for anyone to have
refused him even his rashest desire—so he must be able to
prove to himself that in the end no one did. Yet he was tired,
and hardly wanted the proof; would not want its com-

plications or its disillusionments. And he was virtuous now and ruled a virtuous Court. But still—lest it should be said that he had failed with one mere woman——

Ana laughed—in pity for his confusion of purpose, but making it seem as if she flirted with his gallant remark.

The laugh pleased him, seduced a memory of the days of desire.

"Perhaps they think I was afraid you'd marry again, Ana. After all, they might say that what I could allow to Ruy would not be tolerated in any man less dear to me."

"Then they judge you harshly, Philip, and do me too much honour."

But he was drawing life from her again, and feeling well.

"I wonder, Ana? I am a jealous man, you know—and I have my own ways of being faithful."

Yes, he thought, she is good to be with. She warms a man. And, ruefully his good sense added, she feeds vanity with more grace, more delicacy than courtiers use.

Philip was in his fiftieth year and at a point of immense hesitation and anxiety in his reign. Spain was not merely bankrupt as, despite her stupendous American wealth, she had been since the death of Charles V—but at last her bankruptcy had become Europe's open secret, and it was impossible to foresee how the Council of Finance might re-establish her world-credit. The Netherlands, almost saved to peace and loyalty a year ago by the wisdom of Luis de Requeséns, were plunged in confusion again since his sudden death; one massacre had not solved the Protestant menace in France, where indeed a troublesome Protestant accession to the throne seemed unavoidable now and could only magnify alarmingly Spain's difficulties in northern Europe; meantime the powerful house of Guise, though friendlier to him now than for many years and coaxing for his co-operation in the Catholic League, had to be closely watched—for its great pawn was the prisoner, Mary of Scotland, and any connivance with her party in Europe might throw Elizabeth and England into the scales with William the Silent. Philip was by no means ready to make an enemy of England. Especially with the Mediterranean uneasy, Venice an uncertain ally, the Turk still restive, and the glory of Lepanto seeming far away and indecisive.

In the Peninsula likewise. His cousin, Sebastian of Portugal, clamouring for an insane crusade against Morocco; the *moriscos* making trouble everywhere; the Kingdom of Aragón for ever on the threshold of rebellion; the Church, insinuating and arrogant; the Inquisition always liable to make political embarrassments. The people desperately poor; the politicians suspect, clever and self-seeking; the nobility contemptuous, asleep. And at the Escorial, at home, mountains of work, mountains of writing, little things and big things for ever going wrong and needing his, but always *his*, attention. Sickly children too—and now in late middle age, after four correct marriages, the succession still imperilled. A plain, boring wife who had nothing to say, who obeyed him in everything and encouraged with fanaticism his adopted standards of high, unresting piety; a chaplain, an encircling monastery, a fleet of corporal works of mercy to carry him forward to salvation; and in his breast awareness night and day of the unwinking eye of God.

Yet also, not yet dead, there was all this, for instance. Philip looked uneasily about the beautiful room. There was this plague of beauty and peace—there were all the unregenerate snares that Ana did not even trouble to suggest, but simply stood for.

He pulled a half-dead rose from the bowl beside him.

"You should have a Titian here," he said. "I'll find you one."

She did not answer.

"Titian has died," Philip went on. "Did you hear of his death, Ana?"

"I believe Rodrigo spoke of it. He was extraordinarily old, wasn't he?"

"About a hundred. That is not too old. I hope I live as long."

"But, Philip—why?"

"Because I have so much to do. Oh God, so much. And many, many years will not be enough preparation for death."

His heavy chin was thrust forward. He looked grey and pinched as he stared at the fire. Ana, pitying him and also bored now, smiled a little at her ideas of a moment ago about this pious and worried elderly man. She had no observation to make about death, which she felt confident she would meet tranquilly—with or without preparation—when it came. And she disliked pietistic platitudes. So as kindly as she could she turned the talk to Philip's domestic life.

Yes, the Queen was well; he thanked her. And the little Infantas—his eyes brightened—were very sweet and good. As for the precious, desperately precious small Infante, Diego—he also was fairly well just now. And God would surely heat their prayers, and allow this little child to live?

"The Queen is a saint, Ana."

Ana inclined her head in polite assent. It occurred to her that the span of sanctity was broad, which embraced at once the fiery Mother Teresa and poor, dull Anne of Austria.

"Then things are well at El Escorial—I am glad," she said.

"Oh yes indeed—very well."

"Then why do you suddenly look so sad, my friend?"

He smiled at her kindness.

"I said I missed Ruy," he said. "I always miss him, both as friend and counsellor. But in these months——"

"We hear rumours even here of your new anxieties in the Low Countries."

He looked at her sharply, as if half-offended. Then his gaze turned back to the fire. Silence lay between them for a few seconds.

"Alva's policy was entirely wrong," he said slowly, "and Requeséns has not lived long enough to reverse it. I have need of Ruy, your husband."

Ana did not remind him that nine years ago Ruy had stormed advice at him about the Netherlands—peace, concessions, tolerance, generosity. But Philip had preferred to let the soldier, Alva, have his way. Ruy would have had no new advice now—his advocacy was always for peace and the liberal gesture.

"Rodrigo says they say in Alcala that you are sending your brother now, Don Juan of Austria. Surely that's a good idea? After all, he *is* your father's son—and the Flemings worshipped Charles."

Philip drew himself up in his chair, and she saw with amusement that she had thrust too far into Cabinet secrets.

"They gossip in that University," the king said tartly. "And I'm sorry, Ana, but I cannot talk of state affairs to a woman."

She laughed gently.

"Ruy always did," she said. "You know that."

"I suspected it, certainly. And if he did, he made a mistake."

"It never did you any harm. And I was useful to talk to, as representative of the Castilian nobility, of which neither he nor you know anything from the inside. He always said so."

"You have lost none of your audacity."

"But there's no audacity between friends, Philip, surely?"

He sighed.

"Between friends—no. I know little of friendship now. I have no time for it. And I have no friends."

"You have me."

He laughed.

"I can't afford your friendship, Ana. I am a virtuous king."

"Well, in that case I hope you have some more cheerful

companions about you usually than that gloomy Moor you've brought here with you to-day!"

"Gloomy *Moor!* Be careful, Ana! Are you speaking of Mateo Vasquez, my Secretary of State?"

"Well, Andalusian then! How shockingly he speaks!"

"He is a very learned Canon of Sevilla, and most promising in statesmanship. I cannot have you speak of him with disrespect. He is my right hand. Or is he my left? I don't know which of them I trust the more—he or Antonio Perez. You remember Perez?"

"Yes, indeed—Ruy's best pupil in politics."

"You remember when they used to say that he was really Ruy's bastard son?"

"Lord! All the things they've said, Philip! Whoever 'they' may be!"

They smiled at each other. Ana wondered if Philip was remembering, with her, the days when "they" said that her eldest son, Rodrigo, with his disconcerting golden hair, was Philip's child, and not Ruy's.

"So those are your two great men now," she went on. "A gloomy canon from Sevilla, and a pretty little worldling from somewhere in the wilds of Aragón!"

"Mock as you please, my dear. But they *are* great men. And I agree that Perez is a worldling."

"Ruy always said he'd get to the very top. But I never could see why. He seemed to me to be just a little popinjay—almost a '*mignon*'!"

"No '*mignon*', Perez! He has a wife and family, and other complications too, I hear!"

She laughed outright.

"Astonishing, what women will like! That little silly courtier-boy!"

"He's a man of forty-two, Ana—and the court courts *him*, believe me."

"Forty-two? Six years older than me?"

"Well, forty-two is young in a cabinet minister, but——"

"But in a widow who has had ten children, thirty-six is very old?"

"Let's call it maturity," the king said lightly, and they laughed together. "But I'm forty-nine now, Ana—so, believe me, thirty-six in anyone seems very young to me."

"Ever since I first saw you, when I was eleven, I've thought of you as my contemporary, Philip."

"Dear flatterer!"

"No, I don't flatter. I never learnt how to."

"That's true, I believe."

Philip threw the rose which he had been crumpling on the fire, and pulled another from the bowl.

"Then you will return to Madrid—re-open your house there, Ana? You see the various necessities——"

"Well, truly, I don't—so far. May I think it over, Philip?"

"Of course. But let me have your assent before I leave to-morrow morning, if you please."

"I'll let you have my answer——"

He turned in his chair and looked at her with gravity.

"Shall I perhaps have to *command* you, Ana?"

Before his solemnity she politely suppressed her desire to laugh outright. Was he then becoming a blind autocrat? Did he truly think he could *command* a subject in a private matter?

She avoided answering his foolish question.

"This whiff of the world, this talk with you, tempts me back, Philip," she said. "We have been dull here with our silkworms and our apple-trees."

"They are good things—but they aren't everything. Still, you must come and inspect our orchards at El Escorial."

"I'd love to. But I fear Fernando wants you to visit ours with him to-morrow morning. Would that be possible?"

Philip smiled.

"I shall make it possible. He's a sweet child. Four sons! How lucky you are!"

The fretted, anxious look of Philip the King swept over his face again.

"You are tired now," Ana said. "How very good of you to give all this time to my affairs."

"I promised Ruy to be the guardian of his house. But, believe me, it has been a deep refreshment—just to sit here and talk like this for one hour. I don't know when I've taken such a rest."

"You should do so more often."

"Then, if you think so, come to Madrid, and let me talk to you sometimes."

It was her turn to look at him gravely.

"I expect I shall," she said.

He smiled a little without looking at her. Then he laid his broken rose on the table.

"I must go back to Vasquez and his despatch-box now, I fear."

Ana rose and rang a silver handbell. One of her own manservants entered.

"His Majesty desires to return to his private apartments. Will you send his servants to him here?"

The man bowed and withdrew.

Ana crossed and stood before the fire, looking into it. Her right hand was cupped over her black eye-shade. Philip looked up at her.

"Dear *Tuerta*," he said softly.

She started a little.

"Is there no one left now to give you that nickname?" Philip asked.

"Not since mother died," she said. "But I didn't know you knew——"

"I used to hear Ruy say it——"

"Ah!"

The great walnut door opened again, and two of Philip's servants entered, accompanied by Ana's man.

The king rose from his chair.

"To work then, in God's name," he said.

"The household will have been instructed by Your Majesty's servants as to your wishes about supper," Ana said.

"Yes. Later, later. There is much to do first. But I hope that you will join me at table, Princess? You and the Duke of Pastrana?"

Ana curtsied.

"Your Majesty honours us very much. My son and I will be most happy——"

"Good, good. Till later then, Princess."

She knelt and kissed his hand.

As he crossed the room she thought that his shoulders looked old and pathetic. The servants closed the walnut door.

# PART ONE: *MADRID AND PASTRANA*

## I

BERNARDINA brought wine and placed it on a stone table near the fountain. Antonio Perez rose and made room for her on the bench. It was nearly midnight, and the patio was cool and shadowy.

"The Princess regrets to have to ask you to wait a little, Don Antonio; but she has had an unexpected caller, Don Juan de Escovedo."

"Indeed? Poor Princess! A dullish visitor, I fear?"

Bernardina poured wine into two glasses.

"Yes—he seems a very serious person now. Yet he used to be gay enough—nearly as gay as you were, Don Antonio—in the Prince of Eboli's days, when you were both his protégés. Do you remember?"

"I remember." Antonio looked lazily about the wide, colonnaded patio. "What fun we used to have here then, Bernardina! What parties he gave—dear Ruy!"

"Yes, he was good at parties, Heaven rest him. But so is the Princess. We had some pleasant ones this spring, Don Antonio—even if you *were* sometimes too busy to attend them."

"My misfortune. It isn't all honey, being the king's pet boy, you know, Bernardina."

"I came to know that when you were only a page, my dear. Mother of God, the way Don Ruy had to work!"

Antonio drank his wine, and so did Bernardina.

"He set us an impossible standard. Still—it's very exciting often——"

"And you look a credit to it, if I may make so bold——"

He preened himself amusedly. He was very elegantly dressed and groomed.

"I do my best," he mocked her. "I'm glad you like me, Bernardina."

"I didn't quite say that."

"You did, you old flirt. Anyway, it's clear you like the town, and all our nonsensical goings-on——"

"Ah yes—I like Madrid. I never held with all the pious widowhood at Pastrana—Ana knew I didn't."

"Any more than you held with her mad plan to be a Carmelite nun! Do you remember that fantastic hullabaloo, my dear?"

He laughed and drank again.

Bernardina laughed too, but conspiratorially and gently.

"Dear Ana—what insanity that was! Still, I think I know what was the matter with her then——"

"What *was* the matter?"

"Never you mind, Sir Secretary of State. It's not a Cabinet matter."

"It very nearly was, at the time. The great Mother Teresa will never forgive the Princess, I'm afraid——"

Bernardina chuckled.

"You can hardly wonder. Still—don't ever mention any of that to the Princess."

"I'd hardly be likely to. But why?"

"She doesn't like to remember it—any more than she likes being one-eyed."

"Ah! that!"

"After all," said Bernardina, "we've all made fools of ourselves at one time or another—and she, well, Don Ruy's death frightened her." She sipped her wine. "It's the only time I've seen her lose her head—and I've been her *dueña* since she was eighteen."

Antonio felt vaguely bored.

"She's a very interesting lady," he said.

"She is. What's more, she's good. Ridiculously good—if you want my opinion—in a wicked world."

"Then you're a bad companion for her, I assume?" he said, automatically flirting with this lively middle-aged woman, as he did, inattentively, with anyone who seemed to expect it.

"Yes, I've always made a point of being a bad companion. Ana doesn't mind."

They both laughed.

"Still, hell to this Escovedo! He's making rather a stay, isn't he? Does he often do this?" On the second question he barely veiled his sudden politician's curiosity.

"No—this is only the second time we've seen him. Of course he paid his respects to the Princess at Pastrana in August, just after he got back from the Low Countries—out of devotion to Don Ruy. And we only came back here four days ago, as you know—so we hadn't seen him since."

"He's not much given to calling on ladies——"

"Well, that's no loss to the ladies, let me say. He's grown into a very dull old stick. What's wrong with him? I should have thought that life with Don Juan of Austria would keep *anyone* cheerful! And after all, I expect they *have* a pretty good time, in Brussels and those places? Don't they?"

Antonio laughed very much.

"Oh yes—they're having a simply wonderful time in Brussels, believe you me! The despatches from there are one long, sweet song——"

A door opened at the far end of the patio, and a shaft of light fell through from an inner corridor. Juan de Escovedo came through it, followed by a manservant of the house. As he reached the centre of the patio by the fountain, where moonlight came through from the dark blue sky of Madrid, Antonio stood up and greeted him.

"Good evening, Juan. How are you?"

Juan de Escovedo looked startled—and angry.

"You here?" he said.

"Yes, me. It was a haunt of both of us when we were younger."

"Indeed it was," said Escovedo gravely.

"I was half-expecting you at my office in the Alcazar to-day. I want a talk with you."

"Well, we could go there now—I'm free."

"Ah, but I'm not, my friend. I stop being office-boy at eleven most evenings—if I can. I'm having supper with the Princess."

"Indeed? Then I shan't detain you. Good evening, Doña Bernardina."

"Good evening to you, Don Juan."

"Good evening, Juan," Antonio said, but he received no answer. The servant led him to the outer door. Antonio Perez stood very still and watched him go.

The servant came back across the patio.

"Her Highness will receive you now, sir," he said to Antonio, who turned and bowed to the *dueña*.

"Then I shall say good-evening, Doña Bernardina, and thank you for your very agreeable company."

She lifted her silver cup and leant back in her seat as she smiled at him.

"The pleasure was mine, Mr. Secretary of State," she said lightly. As he followed the servant to the other end of the patio she watched him.

Hardly a man, you'd say, by the look of him—she reflected. But he seems very sure of himself. Well, he has good reason.

She poured herself more wine.


## II

Ana de Mendoza strode up and down the large, formal reception-room in which she waited for Perez. Throughout the day she had been at once amused and on guard about this supper engagement which he had tricked from her—a shade too deftly, she surmised. But now Escovedo's enigmatic and uneasy talk had for the moment overborne flippancy, and she was troubled.

When the servant announced Antonio Perez she came towards him rapidly from the far end of the room, dismissing preoccupation from her face.

Queer to move so fast, he thought. But she has, I suppose, a curious kind of beauty.

He bowed very deeply over her outstretched hand.

"I apologise to have kept you waiting, Don Antonio. But Don Juan's visit was unforeseen—and he is a little—deliberate—of speech."

They laughed.

"Princess, I was of course impatient—but, believe me, I can be impatient very patiently."

"Which is why you are a Secretary of State?"

"No doubt. Still, we have all been openly impatient for your return from the country. Three months has seemed a long time for this house to be shut."

"Yet no doubt you all managed very well when it was shut for three years?"

"Not so well as we do now, Princess, I assure you. Truly, you are an immeasurable asset to Madrid society. Even if it were for no other reason than that it is good for the king to have so dear a friend within reach."

Perez made this speech with tact. Ana observed the well-conveyed sincerity and the careful elimination of any hint of impertinent innuendo. He spoke as one who had no axe to grind and who simply meant what he said. Involuntarily she admired the effect he got, while wondering how much it was calculated.

She had thought this man silly and pretentious when he was young and under her husband's protection. Often she had demurred from Ruy's optimistic view of him. And in the spring just gone—her first season at Court in four years—meeting him first in Philip's company, and afterwards at the

houses of friends and in her own house, she still found it
hard to take him seriously. Yet she knew that, under the
king, he was the most important man in Spain now, and
politically the most intelligent. She saw that his discreet
cultivation of her friendship—its tempo increasing slightly in
the last six weeks, with a chance visit to Pastrana when he was
staying in the neighbourhood in August; then a note with a
gift of books; later his tactful angling to be invited to supper
as soon as possible after her return to Madrid; and yesterday,
flowers, so friendlily labelled: "These are really from the
king, from his precious Aranjuez garden. But may we not
share them? He would like to know that some of them are
with you"—she saw that all this was a political precaution, a
career-manœuvre with its purpose still obscured perhaps
even from himself. But she did not resent it; she knew this
world to which she had come back, and while she remained
in it she was willing to play its game. Until it bored her. It
might do that at any time; but so far she was not bored with
Madrid. She sometimes said to Bernardina that when she had
caught up on its present-day intricacies, when she clearly saw
what all these men of state, clerics and dukes and prelates,
and straight adventurers like Perez, were really pursuing,
when she had the threads of the contemporary situation in
her hands—then she thought she would become bored at
once, and would retreat again, for life, into Pastrana. And
Bernardina retorted that if that was true she would make it
her business to keep her puzzled.

However, she was a long way yet from having any threads
in her hands; and she knew that she was far from fathoming
this odd, successful man who preened himself now so
amusingly before her; as far as she had been a few minutes
earlier from understanding the restlessness and gloom of
Juan de Escovedo. Yet she had seen these two begin their
careers together, she had seen them schooled for the king's
service; and now each wanted something of her—in politics.

Or imagined that in the near future he might. Well—she
would play politics this evening, as she had used to in the
good days with Ruy.

"We are all the king's servants," she replied now to
Perez's polite speech. "But he is so inordinately busy always
that he has very little place left, I think, for such a merely
ornamental thing as friendship."

A servant entered and announced supper.

Antonio extended his hand for Ana's to rest on it, and they
walked together to the supper-room.

"Your friendship would be indeed an ornament on anyone,
Princess," he said as they went. "But the king, who has
enjoyed it so long, knows it for much more than that. He
has a great power of friendship, and he understands, and
indeed he needs it."

Ana looked at him gratefully. She noticed that he often
spoke with gravity and feeling of the king, and that pleased
her. She hoped from her heart that he meant the loyalty his
tone implied.

They sat face to face at table, a low silver dish of many
kinds of sweet-smelling flowers between them. The room
was small and darkly panelled, and lighted by candelabra.
Ana did not allow the servants to stand about while they ate,
but rang for them when they were needed.

"Do you mind?" she asked Antonio. "If you insist on
having poor Juanito rigid at your elbow, say so and he'll do
it——"

"Great Heavens, no!"

"—but I can't stand it. If you talk while they're there as if
they didn't exist or had no ears that's both very rude to them
—and *very* rash. If on the other hand one must discourse all
through supper like an edifying *dueña*——"

"Doña Bernardina, for instance?"

"No, no—my dear and blessed Bernardina—thank Heaven
*she's* not edifying!"

"I imagine not fatiguingly so." His eyes rested on the flowers, and she smiled.

"They smell deliciously—like everything from Aranjuez," she said. "It was very kind of you to share them with me."

"Why, nothing! The gardens at Pastrana can leave you in no lack of flowers. But somehow, as you say, everything from Aranjuez is particularly sweet—so I thought——"

"Thank you very much. But the king is at El Escorial still, isn't he?"

"Yes, indeed. But one of the stewards from Aranjuez was in town yesterday—and the king likes them to scatter his flowers and things among his friends—as *you* must know."

"How he loves his gardens!"

"Yes. It's curious. He's a very complicated man."

"But surely that at least is uncomplicated?"

"That's why I find it complicating."

They both laughed.

"Well, for better or worse, I think he owes it mostly to Ruy—this mania for rural experiment——"

"I think he does. I remember that we youngsters used sometimes to tell Ruy that he should really have been a farmer."

"So did I, often."

"Still, I sometimes wonder now if even Ruy understood what El Escorial was to become?"

"It is the king's darling hobby, isn't it?"

"He's absolutely *mad* about it."

"But that's good for him—makes him happy."

Antonio smiled at her.

"Yes, it makes *him* happy, Princess—and all his happy monks. But some others of his faithful servants could do with less of the simplicities of El Escorial."

Ana had heard that Perez found ways of relieving tedium in the king's mountain hermitage. The queen's ladies-in-waiting were not all as virtuous as the queen. She pretended to misunderstand him.

"But they have the to-and-fro of Secretaries of State and such great people to delight them," she said.

"Well, we do our best," he answered, smiling at her self-mockingly.

"And Rodrigo is growing into a very perfect worldling since he has attended Court up there."

"If I may say so, Princess, Rodrigo was *born* a perfect worldling."

"Yes—isn't it curious? For really neither I nor Ruy was naturally like that."

Perez knew the legend—that Rodrigo was Philip's son. But he could never feel sure that it was true. In spite of the boy's fair hair, he tended to think it as fabulous as that other—that he himself was a bastard son of this woman's husband, Ruy Gomez. Antonio doubted indeed that Ana had ever been the mistress of the king. There had been in Ruy, for all his courtier-skill, a core of self-respect and honour that should have made such a situation intolerable to him. Besides, by all the legends, the king had liked his beauties in the classical and obvious mode. One-eyed and very thin? Perez surveyed his hostess, and wondered. Well—the king's days of pleasure were over, whatever secrets they held. He was pious now. It was a pity perhaps to have become his chief confidant at such a turning point. The hard work the office exacted could have been alleviated by passages of royal laxity—and the Secretary of State would have known how to promote and protect such indulgence.

Perez laughed friendlily about Rodrigo.

"He's very young. Fifteen?" Ana nodded. "And they tell me he shows signs of being a good soldier one day."

"Yes. He's interested in military affairs."

"Has he returned to Madrid with you?"

"No. He's playing about in Andalusia still—with the Medina Sidonias."

"Ah! How is the Duchess?"

Ana's eldest child, now sixteen, was the wife of the Duke of Medina Sidonia.

"Very well, I think. She seems to be beginning to enjoy married life—at last."

The marriage had been contracted when the bride was not yet twelve.

"Well, it should be a success for them. Everyone speaks well of Medina Sidonia."

"Yes—I like him. He's a silly boy—but good-natured and affectionate." She paused and looked grave. In the spring she had agreed to a marriage contract between her third son, Diego, who was only thirteen, and Luisa de Cardenas, ten years his senior. Ana was a traditionalist, and took the practices of the Castilian aristocracy for granted. Yet sometimes in the night—disturbed, whether she recognised this or not, by her own lifelong loneliness—she worried about this marrying-off of children.

She smiled quickly, however, so as not to seem really to mean what she next said.

"We marry them too young. It's a questionable custom."

"Yet—look at you! You were married at eleven, Princess."

"Ah, but I was allowed to continue in childhood until I was nineteen. Besides, Don Antonio, there can be very few men like Ruy. I was fantastically lucky."

"I agree, indeed." But Antonio felt a sudden pang of question and sympathy towards her as he made this polite rejoinder. He wondered what this feeling meant, and it excited him. Meantime he followed her thought of Diego's contract.

"I'm sure Doña Luisa will be fortunate too, however. After all, your son is Duke of Francavilla, and a very charming boy."

Ana laughed.

"She doesn't seem to like his being thirteen," she said.

"That will be remedied. She must be patient."

"Still—I must see, I think, that they don't do that to my two babies—Fernando and the tiny Ana. I'd like *them* to go as they please."

"You're very fond of those two little ones?"

"Yes. Very fond."

"Because they're the babies, no doubt?"

"Oh no. I like them, that's all."

Antonio laughed in surprise.

"That sounds very detached—and unusual," he said.

"I am not particularly maternal," Ana answered coolly. "But Fernando has great charm for me. And Ana—oh, Ana is an angel!"

They rose from the table and went into the corridor and up a minor staircase to the Princess's private apartments. Antonio had not been accorded this privilege before, and he wondered now at the new, odd pleasure which he felt in it, and in the society of this woman whose life, after all, was over.

She's simple almost to dullness, he thought as he moved at her side up the shallow flight of steps. Talks of her children, and of the king's fads, and of the virtues of her dead husband. She isn't witty or formidable in any way, and—wisely—she doesn't play the beauty. What is it then that—by God, that almost moves me?

The candles were dim on the landing, but as the man-servant flung open double doors and light streamed over the threshold of the room they were about to enter, Ana looked at Perez and caught the appraising seriousness of his eyes as they rested on her. She was somewhat surprised by their expression. For she knew, in general terms, why this ambitious man was cultivating her, and that it was by no means for herself. Yet now she saw that at that moment he looked at her—herself; or looked at her as if in search of her.

She crossed the room ahead of him, again with long, quick steps that surprised and vaguely annoyed him.

They seated themselves in two straight-backed, silk-covered chairs near an open window. The servants trimmed the candles, placed wine on a table at Perez's side, and withdrew.

The court-yard below the balcony was very quiet, and all that was visible outside was a low, irregular line of roofs and a bright scattering of stars in the dark blue sky. The sounds of Madrid floated in; clatter of hoofs or wheels, an occasional burst of shrill singing, an occasional shout for the watchman.

Antonio looked with curiosity about the beautiful, long room. There were many pictures, of the Flemish and Italian schools, on the white-painted walls; there was a large writing-table, scattered with papers and seeming as if much used; there were some books piled about; there were flowers and tall candlesticks; there was a graceful daybed which looked as if it came from France; there were figs and apples on a silver dish. A needlework table, ruffled and untidy, stood by the Princess's chair; and a little rag-doll was lying on the floor.

Antonio considered the room as if he were learning something from it. And as he did so Ana considered him, with a more quickened interest than she was yet prepared to recognise.

She knew a great deal about this man, so now she thought she saw what he was thinking as he looked about him.

He was the illegitimate son of Gonzalo Perez and a woman called Maria Tovar. He was born in a village of Aragon, the native country of both his parents. At the time of his birth his father was a student of Holy Orders, not yet ordained. Afterwards, as a priest, he rose rapidly to political power and was a favourite Secretary of State of Charles V, who out of love for him legitimised his son Antonio by imperial diploma. When Gonzalo Perez died, Ruy Gomez became the guardian of this brilliant and promising youth, and supervised his education, first at Alcala and Salamanca and afterwards at Padua. He also trained him in statecraft; and at Ruy's death

Antonio was ready to take his place as leader of the progressive, liberal *amistad*, or party, in Philip's government.

Because of Ruy's affection for him gossips liked to say that he was his son. And because, like Ruy, he was foreign, non-Castilian, energetic and personally ambitious, he was sometimes called "The Portuguese"—as Ruy had been—in lampoons and popular jokes. Ruy had never been more than amused at this would-be jibe, regarding it as a good example of Castilian impudence and insularity; but he had long ago observed to Ana that young Perez secretly hated all such references, and that there was danger for him in his fear of being regarded as anyone's inferior.

Ana surmised that, since Antonio had to be a bastard, he would have chosen to be the son of Ruy rather than of Gonzalo Perez. Not that his true father had lacked distinction, but merely because Gonzalo's greatness had died with Charles V and was a dim story now, whereas the Prince of Eboli had been spectacularly the favourite of the reigning monarch, and one whose name was still a vivid symbol of greatness in Spanish life. Ruy's might have been the more useful paternity—and not the less so because by his marriage he had allied himself to the leaders of Castilian aristocracy.

There, Ana guessed, was the crumpled rose-leaf of Antonio Perez's success. Castile had accepted Ruy, and had even loved him. But it laughed—a vestige too drily, a little too often—at Antonio.

He made mistakes. He was too ostentatiously successful; he dressed over-well, and used—for her taste certainly—too many perfumes and cosmetics; great as was his wealth and power now, his debts were known to be large, and he was said to be venal in office; he paraded his love-affairs, and was inclined to be both charming and insolent on the wrong notes.

More than ten years ago he had married Juana de Coëllo y de Vozmediano. Marriage with this excellent and discreet girl, of impeccable family, should have been a help to him if he truly wished to conquer the amusement of Castilians, and learn to behave as they liked their great men to behave. But Juana, very gentle, fell far too much in love with her husband, and by degrees became blind to all his failings. Moreover, she was domestic and pious by temperament, and shrank from participation in his brilliant and restless public life. She was content to be his wife on his terms, and as such to serve him without question. She was preoccupied too in love and duty towards the children she bore him—one each year, unfailingly.

So he steered his course by his own charting, and although his political acumen was very nearly perfect, socially he continued to make mistakes. And Ana knew that he knew that he made them. But he was proud and impatient, and perhaps felt that he had gone too far by his natural inclinations to change his tactics now. Besides, jealousy was the chief reason why the indolent dukes and marquises of Spain laughed at him. He understood that; he could not fail to. Moreover, he knew that he was impregnably the king's man; knew that, Philip's faith once given, his support and indulgence of a friend could be illimitable; and that in fact he distrusted his weakened aristocracy and preferred to choose his statesmen from outside its ranks.

Still, since the king had almost commanded Ana de Mendoza back into society, it was natural that Perez should renew his friendship with her and her house. Not merely because she was a lifelong friend of the king, and the widow of his own generous patron. These motives were becoming and polite. But Ana knew that they cloaked another. Her name, de Mendoza, represented exactly that element of Spain which baffled him and hurt his self-esteem. But, if he could make her his friend, if he could be known to have her approval, that would be a social victory indeed, a resounding answer to the snobs who were her uncles and her cousins.

After all, she had married an *arriviste*, and been of incalculable
service to his career; she could therefore possibly befriend
another, were he lucky enough to please her.

In general this was the motive, Ana believed, of Perez's
bid for her present friendship. There might be something
more specific, more political, also. With Juan de Escovedo's
conversation in her mind she believed that perhaps there was.
These men had once been close friends, and she gathered that
their friendship was waning now; both believed her to have
influence with the king, and both took some trouble to seek
her out.

She smiled a little. She wondered if Perez would show
anything of his real purposes to-night.

He studied the room too attentively, she thought. He
seemed as if worried by it.

Ana had never entered his own great palace, just round the
corner from her house, in Plaza Santa Maria, but she knew
that it was an almost comic legend of splendour. In the
summer of 1576, when she was still in retirement at Pastrana,
Rodrigo and his flippant young friends used to bring home
crazily amusing tales of the Perez magnificence. Don Juan of
Austria had been staying with the Secretary of State then as
his guest, and there were many parties and receptions, and
Ana had laughed at Rodrigo's reports of tables of solid,
embossed silver, of gold and jewelled dinner services, of
flunkeys in fantastic liveries. And even her sober and kind old
neighbour at Alcala, the Marqués de los Velez, had managed
to be quite amusing when he described Antonio's bedroom.
His bed, it seemed, had posts carved—in silver—in the form
of enormous angels with jewel-eyes and outspread wings.
And there were stars and a crescent moon of jewels, and
hangings of azure and cloth of gold, and perfumes burning in
gold censers, on onyx pedestals. It was no wonder that this
somewhat raw voluptuary did not like El Escorial, with its
whitewash, truckle beds and straw-seated chairs. And now,

no doubt, he was puzzled—if not disappointed—by the ordinariness of her domestic arrangements.

She looked at him gently, and reflected that she liked the light, boyish cut of his face. Not its handsomeness, which was only too obvious, but its alert suggestion behind the charm, its hint of an anxiety that might almost be taken for innocence. He's odd, she thought approvingly; he's himself. He runs quite counter to our usual male conventions. But she did not go on to reflect that this had also been true of the only two men who had ever touched her heart—the king and her husband.

She bent and picked up the little doll.

"I promised Ana that this poor girl should have new underwear," she said.

"She seems to need tidying up."

Ana sorted some pieces on the work-table.

"A *silk* petticoat, I think," she said. "After all, she *is* called Juana La Loca."

Antonio laughed very boyishly.

"After the king's grandmother? Poor girl, poor little doll!"

"Oh, Queen Juana was a wonderful woman, I think—or anyway Anichu does. Would you be so good as to move that candelabra a little nearer?"

He got up and did as he was told. He stood a moment looking down at Ana's bent dark head, and then he looked again about the room. He felt amused and rested. The king's Alcazar, its cabinet rooms and offices so packed with heavy work and shrouded national troubles, was only just across the street, but it suddenly seemed miles away.

As he went back to his chair a bell began to toll at Santa Maria de Almudena.

"How lovely it is here," he said gently. "How peaceful!"

Ana looked up from her doll and her piece of silk.

"Yes. I like this room. Won't you drink some wine?"

"Thank you—I'd love to. And you?"

She nodded and he filled two cups.

"I hope they've chilled it enough," Ana said. "It's good. We get it from Bordeaux."

"It's delicious. But I thought you scorned everything non-Spanish, Princess?"

She laughed.

"In general I pretend to. But Ruy taught me some discrimination—and I agree with him now about our *white* wines. But I love our red ones."

"So do I. Still—even those they do better in France, I fear."

"Perhaps they do. Oh, this poor, collapsing doll!"

"Shall we look for a new Mad Queen for little Ana?"

"No good. She has a passionately faithful heart."

"Ah! Do you think that a good possession, Princess?"

"I hardly know. But I understand it."

Antonio sipped his wine and watched her long hands at their work.

The convent bell dropped away into silence.

"Well," he said suddenly and lightly, "are you going to tell me what Juan de Escovedo was grumbling about?"

She looked at him, put down her sewing and sipped some wine.

"Then we are to talk politics?" she asked.

"Do you know anything about them?"

"I used to. But now I'm out of touch."

"Yet the king comes to see you here, doesn't he?"

"Yes. Usually he sits exactly where you're sitting now."

"Ah! How very much I am honoured!" In passing he wondered if Philip would whole-heartedly approve of the honour being done to him. "I wonder what he talks about to you?"

"Oh, family affairs—these settlements over my father's recent marriage, and my cousin's lawsuit, and so on. And the children and their education."

"It sounds—just a little boring."

They laughed.

"We talk about old times too, about Ruy, and—Queen Isabel. And he tells me how El Escorial is getting on. He comes here to rest, you see."

"He doesn't know how to rest."

"That's true. So sometimes his real preoccupations are hinted at too, although he hates to give anything away."

"But he does. You gather things?"

"Some things. In any case, he isn't after all my only visitor! The Cardinal—and others—sometimes call."

"Including Escovedo."

"Yes. Poor Juan. He's always been devoted to Ruy and all of us. But now he seems to be getting dissatisfied with me—I truly don't know why."

"He's getting dissatisfied with everyone—except Don Juan of Austria. It's very foolish of him."

"But he used to be exceptionally shrewd."

"That's why he was put in charge of Don Juan, who has, as you know, no sense at all. He's a romantic figurehead, and his only use to us in Flanders is that the Flemings like him for being his father's bastard with one of their own women. Escovedo's job was to impose our policy, and keep Curlyhead out of mischief."

"And why is everything going wrong—as I gather it is—in Flanders?"

"You 'gather' only too truly, Princess." Antonio stood up and paced somewhat uncertainly about the room. His face was hard and clouded. "Escovedo is the reason why everything is going wrong again in the Lowlands. That may sound absurd to you—but, believe me, it isn't. Not all the blandishments of His Holiness, nor the half-promises of Guise and the Catholic League, nor the beckonings from Mary of Scotland need stand a second's chance against one well-trained politician at Don Juan's elbow now. They are all straws in the wind against the facts. Your husband, Princess, or I, or Mateo Vasquez—any of us, who are realists, would simply have protected him, mercilessly, against his own absurdity. And Escovedo was a man like us, with our training. I'd have sworn he was equal to this job."

"And why is he failing in it?"

Perez laughed, but half-angrily.

"He is failing in it because—well, one must almost say because he has fallen in love with our Lepanto captain! He has forgotten the king. Don Juan has become his king."

Ana had not the clues to all that lay behind this outburst, but she was prepared to wait for them.

She smiled.

"Then why does he come bothering me?" she asked lightly. "Philip is my king."

Perez thought that as she said this she looked very beautiful. He paused by the table and raised his glass.

"Shall I go on being indiscreet?" he asked her.

"So far there's been no indiscretion—because I do not understand your references. For instance, what has poor Mary of Scotland to do with our mistakes in Flanders? She's still in prison, isn't she?"

"Indeed she is, thank God! And long may she stay there, and merry may she be!"

"Unchivalrous!"

"Realistic. In any case, it's much the safest place for the poor woman."

"But what is she doing in this conversation?"

"Ah, Princess—I don't think I can quite tell you that. That's a whole despatch-boxful of gossip—and very tricky."

He moved away from her, and his face grew hard and angry again. She watched him with interest. He cares about his work, she thought. Ruy would approve of this earnestness. He is not where he has got to entirely, or even much at all, for vainglory—let his enemies say what they will. The splendours are his reward indeed, and he must have great vitality to be able to snatch so greedily at them while giving so much passion to his work. But the passion is there. He is wholly in earnest for Philip and for Spain.

He turned in his walk, flung out his hands and spoke, looking at her indeed, but still as if she were not there, or as if he were alone.

"Parma's had to take the army back to Flanders—you know that? Namur! And Margaret of Navarre! Curlyhead is getting positively literary! And Antwerp now, we gather—and despatches peppered with that dear old *cliché* 'fire and sword'! My God—as if old Alva's blunderings had never happened! As if we'd never heard of the Perpetual Edict! Madam, we slaved for that, the king and I—and the Estates were just beginning to believe in our sincerity. No thanks to Don Juan either that we *did* get it ratified in May. And now it's all in the dust and we're disgraced again in the Lowlands—simply because Escovedo won't control the day-dreams of a soldier-boy!"

"What are these day-dreams?"

"If I told you, Princess, I'd hardly expect you to believe me."

He dropped back into his chair, and smiled at her.

"You don't remember the king's father, do you, Princess?"

"Oh yes, I do. I was seventeen when he died."

"Ah! Well, he was a very great ruler, but he certainly made one mistake. You should never educate an illegitimate prince as if he were legitimate. Old Charles was far too tender towards his favourite bastard."

"Don Juan has great charm. He was a very charming little boy."

"So he is still—a very charming little boy." They laughed, and Perez drank more wine. "But why do I bore you like this? Why am I treating your lovely house as if it were the Cabinet Room?"

"I'm honoured——" Ana murmured amusedly.

"It's Escovedo's fault. Damn him, why does he have to cross my path even when I come to visit you?"

"Poor man, he seems to get on all our nerves."

"Is he on yours too? What was he scolding you about, Princess?"

Ana threaded her needle and began again on the hem of the doll's petticoat.

"A great many things," she said. "Really, if he weren't so much in earnest one would have to call him very impertinent."

"I call him that—and plenty besides."

"So I gather. But he and I aren't on those terms, perhaps——" They laughed—"And then, he *did* love Ruy."

"No more than I did. Not half as much."

Ana raised her head and looked at him. He felt a long surmise in her look, and submitted to it with a pleasure he refused to analyse. Her hands are exquisite, he thought irrelevantly, as he waited for her to speak again.

"Escovedo thinks that it is shocking of me to have forsaken my widow's solitude at Pastrana."

"Has he had the audacity to say so?" Ana nodded. "Well, he always was a rather clumsy kind of prig."

"Yes—but cunning too." Perez raised his brows in a question. "You see," Ana went on, "I think he felt it to be a duty he owed to Ruy to make that clear to me—he has come to see me twice simply to get it said. *But*, he also says that he understands that I have returned to Madrid because the king wished me to. He finds that odd and unwise in the king, he says——"

"You *let* him say these things?" Perez was laughing delightedly now.

"It amused me—and I couldn't stop him. I said nothing. But I think I vaguely saw his—his politics."

"What did you vaguely see, Princess?"

"He wants—urgently—to influence someone who may

have influence with the king. Now, though he disapproves of me at present, he knows me well from the old days, and he thinks that for Ruy's sake I might be persuaded to be of service to him. He always inclined to believe, long ago, that I was the king's mistress—and now I think he is hoping that so I am again—shocking as he finds the idea——"

Silence fell.

In the surface of his mind Antonio was smiling at Escovedo's grotesque manœuvres—but he could not trouble to smile at them outwardly. Indeed he felt his features locked in gravity, for the inner reaches of his mind were swept empty of politics now, and were filled instead with an excitement wholly personal. He recognised it, for he was practised in personal adventure; always unable to forgo its claims. And in the two hours he had been with her this woman had been gaining on his curiosity, on his desire—gently, gently, like a gentle, incoming tide; each soft ripple of surprise slipping over its forerunner irresistibly, yet without hint of force. Her hands, her voice, her dangerous simplicity, her gaunt, almost her ungainly beauty—all had been beckoning him nearer inch by inch to an adventure he dared not risk, but knew—knowing himself—he would now at all costs seek and carry through. And at last she had spoken—lightly indeed, and on a note which baffled him—of the life of her own heart, or at least of what was rumoured of that life. And as he heard her he saw that her daring joke had brought him—ruthlessly and far too soon—to the point his impulses were set upon.

"I have embarrassed you," Ana said.

He did not answer her at once. He pondered the girlish kindness of her voice as it dropped away. I shall regret what I am about to take, he thought.

He leant and took the rag doll from her hands and smiled at it.

"Juana La Loca," he said softly. He got up, still holding the doll, and walked to the window.

"It isn't easy to embarrass me, Princess." He leant against the embrasure and looked back at her and at the quiet room stretching beyond her.

"You always wear black?"

"I am a widow."

"I came here to-night feeling quite correct, quite normal. As if going to dine with the Cardinal, say—or any of the things one does any evening in Madrid. I can remember now exactly how—how usual I felt, as I talked with Doña Bernardina in the patio."

Ana smiled a little.

"You are still entirely yourself, I think."

"Yes. I don't lose myself—ever. Suddenly seeing what you have to do, suddenly being seized by a new intention — that isn't getting lost."

Ana leant back in her chair so that her face was lifted into the candle-light. It seemed exaggeratedly long and white; the black silk patch lay close and sad along her right cheekbone. Antonio appraised her calmly, shackled to his passionate intention.

"No," Ana said. "I suppose that isn't getting lost—or needn't be."

He came and stood by her chair.

"Then you understand what has happened to me? You know what I am going to ask?"

"It's I who'll ask," she said. "Make no mistake—it's I who'll do the asking."

She spoke very quietly, but in new sensitiveness he heard her words as if they were a hard, imperative call. I have no clue to her, he told himself admonitorily; I have no light. What is this coolness that I have never met before? What is this mad tranquillity?

He thought of the king, and even wondered if he was asleep then in his narrow bed at El Escorial—or praying, perhaps? Pray for me, Philip; pray for your servant. He laid the rag doll on a stool and took Ana's hand.

"Are you thinking of the king?" she asked.

"How did you know?"

"You're very near me—it seems natural to see what you think."

Antonio laughed. He had a sudden long view of what he and Ana were about to risk; he saw their future actions as from all angles at once, worldly, sensual and moral, and the vision made him laugh aloud against his own panic. "We'll have good reason to."

She looked down at their joined hands, considering them, it seemed to him, as if they were the hands of strangers. "I wonder what you really want from me," she said.

"So do I," he said. "I think I want the chance to find that out."

"You ask a lot."

"I do."

"I'm very grateful to you."

An hour ago, she thought, perhaps five minutes ago I hadn't even imagined this which I am now about to take. And I don't know that I want it. But I want to find that out.

"You say disconcerting things," said Perez.

"There's no need really to say anything."

"I agree. Still—there's something on the tip of your tongue?"

"Yes. Something unwise. It's only this. I'm nearly thirty-seven, and I'm said to have had more power in my hands sometimes than any woman in Spain. Yet this is only the second time in my life that I've decided anything for myself."

"When was the other time?"

She bit her lip, and Perez felt her hand tighten against his.

"That was a mistake," she said.

He was touched by the droop of her shoulders as she spoke. He fell on his knees before her.

He smells like a woman, she thought amusedly—like a very expensive and fastidious woman.

Yet her attention was not wholly his, for she had reminded herself of Ruy in his coffin, and of the Discalced Carmelites singing, as they had used to, in her convent at Pastrana. But that was absurd, she thought; that was beyond my strength. Coldly she shut Mother Teresa from her thought, and laid her hand upon Antonio's scented hair. I'm only seeking pleasure now, she told herself, and as she bent above her lover she smiled again—in surprise at her situation. But more than at that she smiled at her sense of inexperience.

THE SECOND CHAPTER      (DECEMBER 1577)

I

Bernardina Cavero hated riding and hated cold weather. But she liked to see life, and she agreed with Ana that it was more easily viewed from a saddle than from within a coach. Also she derived much entertainment in these days from close observation of her mistress. Ana rode a beautiful Andalucian mare, a roan, whose cavortings had no influence at all on the *dueña's* stolid mount, a heavy Castilian beast of great reliability.

"I don't know how you tolerate that exhausted old battle-charger," Ana said. "He must be most fatiguing. No, children! Ana, Fernando! Don't you hear me? We're going home now! Ride ahead of them, Jaime," she said to the groom at her side, "and round them up."

"Thank God!" said Bernardina. "How I loathe physical exercise."

"You'd get enormous if it wasn't for me," said Ana.

"Yes. Wouldn't that be restful?"

The two children, on small clipped mules, came cantering back with Jaime, their harness bells jingling.

"But we didn't even get as far as St. Joseph's well," Fernando grumbled.

"Next time," said Ana. The two little riders looked sweet and rosy, tight-packed in dark velvet and fur. "Poor Bernardina's nose is almost falling off with cold—look! And you know I swore to Nurse that you'd be in before the Angelus."

The party swung their horses out of the Retiro Wood and towards the half-frozen high road. They passed other riders, many of whom bowed ceremoniously to Ana, or looked admiringly at her or at the children. The trees stood stiff in winter armour; voices and hoofs rang clearly through the frosty quiet.

"It'd be lovely to go on riding here long after dark," said Ana.

"Let's do it!" said Fernando.

"God forbid!" said Bernardina.

"Alas! We can't, Fernán," his mother said. "We have to lead respectable lives."

"What's 'respectable'?" said little Ana.

"Well—you are, darling."

"It's because we know the king so well," Fernando explained to his sister. "There, Mother!" He pointed with his whip down an avenue of the wood. "There's the place where you first met the king—didn't you—when you were a little girl?"

"Yes—just along there. But he was only a prince then. And he was riding with your father."

"And you were riding with *your* father," said little Ana.

Bernardina and Ana laughed to each other, for that piece of conversation was a ritual of every return from the Retiro with these two children.

"I wonder when *you'll* meet a husband and a prince in the wood, Baby Ana?" Bernardina said.

"Any day now," said Anichu.

They rode into Madrid by the east gate, the Puerta del Sol. The open square was crowded and noisy; it was still clear day, but there were lights already in some windows, and the chestnut men were out with their braziers. Jaime and the second groom edged the party together and flanked it carefully.

"I'd love some chestnuts," said Fernando.

"Nonsense," said Bernardina. "There are loads of them at home."

"But they don't roast them so well at home—are we going by the Plaza Mayor, Mother?"

"If you like, darling."

"And just down to the Cebada Market for a minute?" said little Ana.

"Oh, that's a bit far, my pet?"

"Just to the little almond-paste woman?"

"All right, greedy—but what terrible greedies you are!"

"Anyone would think there wasn't a crumb of anything in the house," said Bernardina. "And of course it doesn't matter at all if I get a death-colic from this cold——"

"Well, let's ride faster and get warm," said Ana.

They trotted through the Plaza Mayor and by narrow, crowded streets to the gay market. The almond-paste dealer brought her trays to them, and Anichu and Fernando chose some little men and women made of nougat. The old woman kissed the children, Bernardina paid her for the sweets, and Ana smiled at her and thanked her.

"I think she's her own model for those little men and women," Ana said as they rode away.

"I expect so," Anichu said gravely, studying one of the nougat figures with care before she licked it.

In the Calle Mayor, where the great merchants had their shops, a fat man in a doorway bowed almost to the ground in salutation to the Princess.

Ana reined in her mare a little.

"Jaime, tell Don Pedro Garcia that I expect him at the palace at noon to-morrow."

Jaime rode to the kerb, and the cavalcade slowed down.

Bernardina eyed Ana gravely.

"I hear from Diego—and others," she said, "that Garcia is more unscrupulous than any jeweller in Paris—let alone in Spain."

"He *knows* about jewels," Ana said.

"They're certainly a new fad of yours, my dear."

"Oh, *I* don't care for them particularly; as you know, I never did," said Ana coolly.

Jaime returned and bowed to his mistress, and the horses fell into a trot again.

Bernardina tried not to smile too appreciatively, but she liked audacity, and she was alert to the game which, without a word said as to its rules, she and Ana had engaged upon this winter. The scandalous fact which underlay their game excited, and sometimes frightened her. She knew more about it, she hoped, than any person in Madrid besides the two whom it so passionately involved; but until Ana spoke of it to her, she knew that she must give no sign. Yet clearly Ana knew that her *dueña* knew the mad thing she was doing, and one day she would talk of it with her; for she had no other *confidante*, and their years together had surely made them trust each other?

Bernardina was not high-principled or committed to ideals of loyalty. Rather, she was a gossipy woman, discreetly loose and sympathetic to looseness. She came from the south, and mocked at the rigidities and etiquette of Castile; the religiosity in high life around the king she found ridiculous, and, without malice, but simply because her cynical and sensual nature preferred life thus, she liked to perceive betrayals, into fleshiness, into venality, into what you will of sin, among these thin-lipped aristocrats. But she knew her place and her duty; and if she was shrewd she was also kind towards her fellows in general.

To Ana, however, she had long since given affection. She was forty-eight now and in her twentieth year of service with the Princess; her husband was employed as a clerk on the Pastrana estates and as assistant tutor to Ana's sons; her only child was being trained as a bailiff at Pastrana; thus her chief interests ran through the pattern of Ana's. Ruy Gomez had been a good employer, and Ana carried on the government of his household as he had designed it; so Bernardina was content with her position in life, and naturally had grown attached to her benefactress. But more than that—she persistently found Ana enigmatic to a degree which she was too lazy to measure, but which kept in their association a touch of question and wonder that was novel for Bernardina.

Ana often maddened her; often she had felt contempt for the girlish unadventurousness with which she rode past occasions of adventure; often she had gasped in sheer, vulgar astonishment before the story-book Castilianism of Ana de Mendoza and that great lady's comical unconsciousness of her own absurdity; often she had thought that the brilliant Ruy Gomez was, domestically at least, the most complacent ass in history. Yet she loved them both increasingly with the years, and she enjoyed, maliciously and kindly, the close view of the great world which their life allowed her. And always Ana, not knowing what she did, kept the hint of question, of surmise astir. In her happiness and afterwards, at Ruy's death, in her foolishly misdirected grief, in her virtue, in her simplicity, she always seemed to Bernardina—who could hardly formulate the fancy, indeed—as if waiting, or as if unexpressed; as if there was something in her forgotten or mislaid, in the lack of which she might never be truly explained.

This hint conveyed itself to Bernardina more as a sensation than a thought—and she had found it somewhat foolish in herself, as if she were inclining to the poetic or the mock-melancholy about a life which lacked for nothing, about a woman who was only not spoilt because, in her naïve arrogance, she was beyond the power of spoilers. Yet the sensation was constant, and bred a kind of tenderness, a fixed indulgence in the *dueña*, which by now was love indeed, and so proceeded, of its nature, to loyalty. Love and loyalty unexpressed, and hardly shaped into a thought—for Bernardina was laconic, and preferred to amuse than to caress.

But now there was no occasion for mock-melancholy. Now, when it was almost too late, the scatheless and self-sufficient aristocrat had paused for a human commonplace, had allowed it to overtake her. Bernardina ought to have been pleased, and often told herself she was pleased. She preferred love-affairs to virtue; she liked intrigue and disliked austerity; she had always desired that Ana might enjoy herself on what she considered natural terms, and through the sweets of normal weakness.

Yet, if possible what had happened was *too* normal? At first Bernardina had approved cold-bloodedly—though in vast surprise—of what she perceived. The thing was begun in caprice, she would swear, and was pursued by some very private form of calculation—in cool pursuit of pleasure. Whether because pleasure was an unknown country, or having been lost must be trodden once more before the end, Bernardina could not guess. But pleasure was Ana's quarry a month or two ago. And for the man who brought it to her? Pleasure of the senses yes, and another kind of personal satisfaction too. Something to do with pride and politics and the love of danger and the need to prove his grasp on his every smallest worldly whim.

But now—the man was impassioned, infatuated. And Bernardina, who knew much about his secret life, surmised empirically from it and from the degree of his present frenzy that he would have burnt up every cinder of this desire within, at best, a year from now. Unless indeed the fabulous generosity and greatness of the lady could keep his worldliness entranced—but that would not be passion, let him simulate with all his skill.

No matter. These things were better brief and hot. Safer too. There could be no hope of secrecy. Servants were doubtless on the nod and wink already—great Heavens, what did Ana think that they were made of? But the Eboli servants liked on the whole to retain their posts, and Bernardina guessed that if an indiscretion of their mistress did not go too far or last too long, they and their talk would be manageable. And short-lived scandals seldom did much harm. If they did, where would any of us be? thought the *dueña*.

Thus she debated often nowadays, and reassured herself—and enjoyed her own common sense and its conclusions.

But a shadow moved below these, its shape evading her. A new kind of hint about her mistress teased her now, and even, in her less guarded moments, made her angry. For Ana was no longer as she had been in September and October. She was not at the beck of pleasure now. She was in love, Bernardina believed; and what so strangely mettled a creature would make of that condition the *dueña* had no means of guessing. But she was not romantic and she feared the prospect. Moreover, at present it sometimes seemed to her that whatever Ana might henceforward make of love, love already had the power almost to make her seem ridiculous.

"God bless you, Bernardina! That was a terrible sneeze!"

"Rodrigo says Bernardina's is the loudest sneeze in Madrid," said Fernando. "Did you know that, Mother?"

The Angelus, which rang at sunset in Madrid, sounded from Santa Maria Almundena.

"There, we're late," said Ana.

The entire life of the street paused at the bell, and the cavalcade with it. Everyone made the sign of the Cross and said the customary "Hail Marys" and a prayer for the faithful departed. The horses were reined in for this on the corner of Plaza Santa Maria and Calle Segovia.

Bernardina smiled as she prayed, for they were drawn up at the very porch of Antonio Perez's palace. A fine place for this family to be saying the Angelus, she thought, and glanced at Ana to see if she was smiling, but found that her face was perfectly composed.

As they rode across the Plaza, Anichu pointed back to the house they had just passed.

"Doña Juana lives there with Don Antonio," she said.

"They have a tremendous lot of children," said Fernando.

"Yes," said Anichu. "And they have one tiny, tiny one— I saw it. It's so tiny I don't think it can open its eyes yet. Why don't you have a little one like that, Mama?"

"I'm too old, Anichu. Anyway, *you* finished me. You were the last straw, my precious baby."

They rode through the gateway of the Pastrana palace, and dismounted in the court-yard.

## II

Antonio Perez threw more wood on the bright fire and then bent to warm his hands. He had just left the king's workroom after a long conference, and his own office cheered him by contrast. Philip is an uncomfortable poor devil, he thought. He rang a handbell, and moved towards his writing-table.

"Bring some wine," he said to the servant, "and tell them to send me in something to eat later on. Something simple that won't delay me—a sausage or something, and some bread. And have I plenty of candles? I shall be here late to-night."

He sat down to work. Despatch-boxes were stacked on shelves by his side; the table was strewn with papers. He trimmed the candle nearest him and began to cut some quills.

The Cabinet meeting in the morning had been long and tricky; in the early afternoon he had got through much work with his secretaries; at five o'clock Philip had sent for him, and the ensuing three hours' debate meant—as did almost all private sessions with the king—secret and troublesome readjustment of many decisions painfully reached with the Cabinet.

I shall be here half the night, he reflected. Ah, but she likes the small hours; she suits me well in that. He smiled—a very brilliant, contented smile. Then he thought with pitying amusement of Mateo Vasquez, whom he had met a moment ago in the corridor—on his way in his turn to Philip's room. Vasquez, a very earnest priest, was Perez's rival in the Cabinet for Philip's confidence. Poor Mateo! If he's only *going* into conference now he'll certainly be working until breakfast-time. Good for his vow of celibacy. And now in the next three hours Philip will rescind with Mateo, or *pretend* to rescind, everything he and I have just pretended to settle. And when I send him to-night's memoranda in the morning, they'll all come back covered with marginal second thoughts—arising from talk with Mateo. But *I* won't be told that, of course. It's miraculous that we manage, between us, to keep his kingdom in motion at all!

The pens were ready. He chose one, and settled to work. In a minute he was engrossed in re-drafting a very private despatch to the new ambassador in Paris, de Vargas Mejia. He might joke about the multiplicity of his labours, but he loved the work and had a very fine grasp on Philip's peculiar and devious foreign policy. He gave it industrious attention, and never allowed his strong bent for pleasure to deflect him from the business of the State.

He worked in peace for more than an hour. He got up sometimes to search in files, or merely to pace about the room, or stand and stare into the fire. Sometimes he took a mouthful of bread from the tray they had brought him;

sometimes he chewed absent-mindedly at a chicken-leg. Then back to his table, to a new pen and the State paper spread before him.

When he heard the door open he did not look up at once. None of his clerks was in the Alcázar at this hour—it could only be a boy to attend to the fire. But he did not care to have people fussing round, so when he came to the end of a note he lifted his head, feeling impatient.

Juan de Escovedo was standing at the other side of the table.

"'Escoda' in person!" said Perez, and was pleased to see the other start at hearing that appellation. "'Escoda' un-announced—and indeed uninvited! How did you get admitted to my room at this hour, may I ask?"

"Don't be silly," said Escovedo shortly. "Every servant in the Alcázar knows *me.*"

"Yes, but they know me too, and know that to disobey my orders is a quick way to lose a good job."

"You're getting very arrogant, Antonio."

"Am I?" He paused to pour some wine. "Perhaps I am. Will you drink?"

Escovedo shook his head. He stood rigidly, his dark, long face unrelaxed and solemn. Perez eyed him with calculation and dislike. He was a most unwelcome visitor, all the more unwelcome because he was in these months a very great weight on the mind of the Secretary of State. But now he was here, might it not be useful to Philip to make one clear, firm appeal to whatever was left of political judgment in this man?

As he pondered this and his possible approach to any such appeal, he carefully folded and covered all the papers on the desk, and closed the lids of despatch-boxes.

Escovedo almost smiled as he watched him.

"No need for that, Antonio. I haven't your skill in reading other people's letters."

"I believe not. Still, I take no risks, 'Escoda'. You don't

like my making free with your new Papal pet-name? Ah well, you see the fact that I can, is proof that Pope Gregory and his ambassador aren't as tidy with their desks as I am with mine——"

"We all know your methods——"

"Yes, I'm thorough. I get to know everything. But you ought to have remembered that sooner, Juan."

Escovedo drew himself up to a still greater rigidity, and spoke with fanatical and solemn disgust.

"You have become an entirely corrupt and dishonourable man, Antonio Perez."

Perez leant back in his chair and smiled.

"For one who, during at least two years, has plotted in consistent dishonour against his king, who made him whatever he is, and to whom he owes everything, that's an audacious and comic pronouncement."

Escovedo waved the comment off.

"I've come to talk to you of private matters."

"I don't give a curse what you've come to talk about. You've no business coming here at all at this hour, and without appointment. But now that you are here, you'll talk about whatever I choose. And first, will you be so good as to sit down?"

Escovedo shook his head.

"No? Then I'll stand up. No need to get a stiff neck from looking at you." He rose, walked to the fire and threw a log on it. When he turned his face again to Escovedo its expression had altered. He looked boyish and serious.

"Juan," he said, "we used to be friends. And we learnt our profession together, from the best of all masters." Escovedo drew in a sharp breath, as if in pain, but Antonio went on talking. "Before I go into any of the politics of this mess you're making, therefore, I'm going to give you some strictly personal instructions—and they are exactly what he, Ruy Gomez, would give you——"

"Will you in God's name keep *that* name off your lips?"

"Don't be such a fool! Listen to me, Juan. Before God I ask you to listen now—for *your own sake*. There are three things that you *must* do: (*a*) Write no more of those insane letters to the king; (*b*) resign at once from the service of Don Juan; (*c*) retire to the country, and live a private life for at least five years. Will you—for *your own sake*, man!—undertake to do those three simple things, and do them at once?"

"Please save your breath. I repeat that I have not come here to discuss my political work with you."

"Your political work! Oh God!" Antonio moved uneasily about the room, then came back and faced Escovedo again. "Then you persist? You commit yourself to a planned course of—treason?"

Treason was a dangerous word at Philip's Court. Sinister memories and rumours drooped about it. Therefore Antonio used it now deliberately. It produced an effect.

"Treason? To differ from *your* party in the Cabinet as to policy in the Netherlands isn't treason, Perez. I serve Spain as I was commissioned to; in promoting the legitimate and valiant projects of Don Juan of Austria."

"Legitimate projects of a bastard!"

"You are a bastard, Perez."

"Yes—but a commoner. So I can't howl for the canopy and insignia of a legitimate prince of Spain—like your precious Don Juan! And by the way, he can have his canopy and insignia—though without a vestige of title to them—any time he likes, if he'll just have the grace to try to please his long-suffering brother in one or two matters of State. Philip is nothing if not indulgent to his relatives! But to come back to the point—we were talking of treason, Juan——"

"You were."

"Yes—I was. Now look here—you know, because I've told you so plainly again and again, and so has the king, more circuitously—you know that here in this Alcázar we know all your plots and European negotiatings probably as soon as you know them yourselves. I'm not going to go on about 'treason' now, because it's merely childish to pretend that Don Juan's dreams aren't just a flaming challenge to the king. I merely used the word so that you may know that it's being used here about your activities—and so warned, you can proceed as you like. But I propose to talk policy for a minute——" Escovedo moved impatiently—"and you're going to listen.

"Firstly: we are having peace in the Netherlands. You've smashed that up for us this summer, but, believe me, we are getting it back. Thanks to Juan's recent nonsensical 'victories', we may indeed have to send Parma back with some troops to police the place awhile, as you seem to have it in wonderful confusion. But as you know, a commission is on its way to Brussels now, to re-establish the Perpetual Edict at all costs. And the Estates are going to be asked to choose a new governor—you know all that?—instead of our precious Juan. They are to have anyone they like—probably one of their beloved Archdukes from the Holy Roman— there's Matthais or Ferdinand—oh, they're to have their pick. And our armies are coming home, and there is to be peace."

Escovedo smiled quietly.

"Juan knows the armies—you don't."

"You say a thing like that, and then object to the word 'treason'! By God, man, you must trust insanely to our old affection! Meantime, no matter who knows the armies, Philip pays them, and he will pay them no longer. So much, then, for the Netherlands, and your disastrous efforts there.

"Now, the next thing: we are having no chivalrous volunteering into France, if you please, and absolutely *no* tomfool offers of Spanish troops to the Duke of Guise! Will you once more and firmly instruct Don Juan as to that! Why, Guise hasn't even asked for his assistance—and he's far too wily to risk exasperating Philip at this juncture.

We are keeping out of France's private affairs—understand?"

"A holy war is the affair of any Christian!"

"A holy war?" Antonio laughed. "Oh Juan, what's happened to your old acumen? What has Curlyhead *done* to you? But 'holy war' leads me neatly up to our last and strongest prohibition. Listen, my friend. Don Juan's invasion of England will not take place. That, as you know, was settled years ago. The king *did* consider it at one time, uncertainly and in my opinion *madly*. But he won't have it now at any price, is that clear? And he's very angry at this new and much extended revival of the plan. Oh yes! We know all about the new offers! The Pope's blessing and the Pope's money and the Pope's men! We know that our Charmer is to set free Mary of Scotland and marry her and become King of Scotland. We know that he is to sunder all England and restore it to the Faith; and capture Elizabeth, of course, and give *her* a turn in Sheffield Castle. A 'holy war', indeed. Upon my oath, Juan, it's the most wonderful daydream that has *ever* come to my attention. It's so wonderful because it doesn't bear the remotest relation to existent political facts, or trends, in England or Scotland or any part of Northern Europe. It really is the perfect dream. For one thing—it would enchant the Netherlands, because at its first move it would drive Elizabeth and all England straight into the outstretched arms of the Prince of Orange. France would be ravished with joy at what she would rightly foresee as the end of Spain; the Holy Roman Empire would be magnificently amused. And Elizabeth—before you imprisoned her —well, Elizabeth would just defeat you, Juan."

"You are absurd and cynical," said Escovedo. "Worst of all, as Spain's Minister of State, you are shockingly indifferent to her spiritual responsibility in Europe. But if you *will* discuss what you clearly refuse to examine impartially——"

"I've been examining it for the last two years! You've forced me to. You've wasted more of our time here, and caused Philip more anxiety than any other one problem in external affairs. The king has been extraordinarily patient. He loves Juan, and he has wanted to give him his head, and let him test his own ambitions and find his place in government. But no one could have foreseen this development of blind, supernatural vanity, or—worse still—the power of that vanity to unhinge the judgment of a trained man of politics like you. However, I have warned you, for the last time. And if these lunatic plottings go an inch further I take no responsibility for your fate, or Don Juan's. Philip is extremely embittered against you—far more so than he will let you see just yet. But you know his methods in anger. I don't have to tell *you* anything about the complicated character of the king."

"You talk as if you owned the king," said Escovedo. "But I am openly here in Madrid as Don Juan's emissary to him. I am here to argue with him the advisability for Spain of certain actions we propose in Northern Europe. I see Philip fairly often, as you know, and I am in correspondence with him. I know his character well, and I know therefore that he is probably at present more strongly opposed to my propositions than he lets me see. I even accept your view that he is very angry with us just now, and that therefore my career, and Don Juan's, and even our lives, may be in danger."

When Escovedo said that the two men looked at each other steadily.

"Go on," said Perez.

"But it is my duty to plead this cause, and to pit my conviction against yours. Philip is, after all, a man of deep religious faith—that is where your influence ceases to count, and mine begins. I may not influence him directly, but I can find those who can. Naturally, since we are neither of us 'treasonous', Don Juan and I realise that we can only undertake what we see to do when Philip grants us his blessing, or at least his tolerance. But if he does, he will live to rejoice in

the event, and we shall be content to lay all the honour before
His Majesty. But he has a clear duty now to the Eternal
Faith—and Don Juan is God's instrument, waiting to his
hand."

Antonio Perez looked about the room as if totally at a loss
for means of expression. Slowly he poured more wine and
sipped it slowly.

"Eloquent and idealistic," he said after a pause. "But
unluckily I have done more deciphering than you know. I
didn't sketch out the whole of Don Juan's dream to you just
now. There is an epilogue. When Juan is King of Scotland
and England, and Elizabeth is in the Tower, he plans to have
more to do than be embraced by the Pope and enjoy the
celebrated pleasures of Mary's bed. There is a codicil—
something about bringing all your new great armies and
fleets from the north to Santander, and undertaking to rescue
Spain from the inertia and cynicism of her present ruler.
That has all been noted down in my private archives, Juan."

Escovedo flung his arms apart.

"And it isn't true!" he cried. "It's been flung in my face
before, that vile and senseless tale! There is *no* plot against
the king, never has been, never will be!"

"I've seen it in writing."

"Not in mine—or his! Oh, Don Juan gets angry sometimes! Who wouldn't, with the king's eternal evasions and
delays! And I've heard him lose his temper very indiscreetly,
and say senseless things, of being the better ruler for Spain,
and of invading, and so on. But those were only the briefest
and silliest moments of exasperation. Even so, I have
reproved him for them—and I have feared that they were
overheard."

"Such things creep into ambassadors' reports, and into
despatches you know nothing of, 'Escoda'."

"And if they do, *you* should know how to value them. You
are cynical and corrupt and opportunist now, as we all know

—and you are Philip's most corroding influence, from which it has become imperative to rouse and rescue him. Him and Spain. But you *are* astute—and you cannot fool yourself about my loyalty to the person of the king. You cannot, Perez!"

"In my work I never calculate on persons, as apart from what I see them do. A person more or less is of no account in state affairs—it is what he promotes and what he does that I have to reckon with. I see your recent actions and your future intentions, and I hold them to be invidious. So I am not interested in emotional recollections of the kind of person you are, or seemed to be. I only work on what I see you doing. And I intend to put an end to what you are doing now—because that is my duty. You're a brave man, and I used to think you intelligent, and I used to like you. But your present performances in statecraft are a danger to Spain—and so they will be stopped. I am not sentimental, Juan."

"No, you are *not* sentimental. And that brings me to *my* business here."

"You have no business here that isn't now concluded. I have given you my last instruction. Henceforward you know what is required of you—and you have been warned of the king's extreme displeasure. So good night. I'm very busy."

Perez walked back to his table and sat down.

Escovedo did not move.

"I shall say what I came here to say," he said. Perez did not look up from his work. "I have discovered that you are the lover of the Princess of Eboli."

Perez looked up now, in well-calculated amazement.

"You have what?"

"You heard me."

"Indeed I did." Antonio lay back in his chair and laughed. "I heard you, you scurrilous old woman you!" He paused. "I have been a Secretary of State for eleven years now. For